"Who are you?"

Vince looked down into clear green eyes like pale jade marbles. He backed up a step from the door.

"I'm, uh, Vincent Cutler. You left a message on my—"

"Well, it's about time!" she exclaimed, and bent to grab a shopping bag by the door. "I've got a whole bag full of your mail here."

He looked past her. She'd done wonders with his old place. The apartment had a homey, put-together feel about it that he quite liked.

"Sorry about this. I don't mind coming after it again, if you'll just call. Here's my card."

"I'll send it. So long, Vince Cutler."

"Wait a sec. I'd like to know your name, at least." He smiled.

She considered a moment. "Jolie Kay Wheeler."

His smile stretched into a grin. "Good night. Jolie Kay Wheeler. Maybe I'll see you around."

He didn't know why, but even as that door closed to him, he knew somehow that he hadn't seen the last of spunky, pretty Jolie Wheeler. Strangely enough, that thought was quite all right by him.

Books by Arlene James

Love Inspired

*The Perfect Wedding #3
*An Old-Fashioned Love #9
*A Wife Worth Waiting For #14
*With Baby in Mind #21
The Heart's Voice #261
To Heal a Heart #285
Deck the Halls #321

*Everyday Miracles

ARLENE JAMES

says, "Camp meetings, mission work and the church where my parents and grandparents were prominent members permeate my Oklahoma childhood memories. It was a golden time, which sustains me yet. However, only as a young, widowed mother did I truly begin growing in my personal relationship with the Lord. Through adversity, He blessed me in countless ways, one of which is a second marriage so loving and romantic it still feels like courtship!"

The author of over sixty novels, Arlene James now resides outside of Dallas, Texas, with her husband. Arlene says, "The rewards of motherhood have indeed been extraordinary for me. Yet I've looked forward to this new stage of my life." Her need to write is greater than ever, a fact that frankly amazes her, as she's been at it since the eighth grade!

DECK THE HALLS

ARLENE JAMES

Steeple
Hill®

Published by Steeple Hill Books™

STEEPLE HILL BOOKS

Steeple Hill®

ISBN 0-373-87331-X

DECK THE HALLS

Copyright © 2005 by Deborah Rather

www.SteepleHill.com

Printed in U.S.A.

Show me Your ways, O LORD;
Teach me Your paths.
—*Psalms* 25:4

For my husband, who has taught me how real
and rewarding love can be.

Chapter One

The voice on the answering machine, while obviously feminine, sounded curt and cheeky.

"Come to your old apartment and get your mail before I trash it. Never heard of mail forwarding?"

Vince smacked the heel of one hand against his forehead. Where was his brain? He hadn't given a single thought to having his personal mail forwarded. In the past few weeks he'd been too busy settling into the new house, replacing his business accountant and hiring enough mechanics to fulfill a city maintenance contract to think about his personal mail.

Just about everything important came to the offices of Cutler Automotive, but that was no excuse. He should've realized that the new tenant of his old apartment would have to deal with his share of circulars and the other junk that routinely clogged every mailbox in the Dallas/Fort Worth Metroplex. Besides, something important did occasionally find its way into his residential mailbox. In fact, the materials he'd been expecting about the spring singles' retreat at his church would undoubtedly be among the papers waiting for him at the old apartment.

He hit a button and listened to the message again. Her irritation couldn't have been more obvious, but he found himself smiling at the huskiness of her voice melded with the tartness of her tone. He heard both strength and vulnerability there, an odd combination of toughness and femininity. Since he was still wearing his jacket over his work clothes, he decided that he might as well go at once, make his apologies and relieve her of the unwanted burden of his mail.

Picking up his keys from the counter, he jauntily tossed them into the air, snatched them back again and retraced his steps through the new, sparsely furnished house to the garage and the shiny, white, three-quarter-ton pickup truck waiting there. Glancing at the sign proudly painted on the door, he climbed inside and started it up. The powerful engine rumbled throatily for a moment before he backed the truck out onto the drive and in to the street.

As he shifted the transmission into a forward gear he tossed a wave at his next-door neighbor Steve, who was taking advantage of the clear, early-November weather in the last hour of daylight to walk his dog. The Boltons were nice people. Wendy, the missus, had been one of the first people to welcome Vince to the neighborhood. They were about his age and the proud parents of a sixteen-month-old curly-top named Mandy, who took most of their time and attention, but Wendy seemed determined to "fix him up" with one of her single friends. Steve had confided that his wife found Vince too "tall, dark and delish" to be still single at twenty-nine, but that she'd have felt the same way if he'd been a "bald warthog."

Vince didn't know about being "tall, dark and de-lish," but he didn't think he was a "bald warthog," ei-ther. He'd happily give up the single state the moment that God brought the right woman into his life. So far he hadn't stumbled across her—not that he'd exactly been out beating the bushes for the future Mrs. Cutler.

He was a busy man with a booming business, three garages and a large extended family, including his par-ents, four sisters and half a dozen nieces and nephews, with one more on the way, not to mention the brothers-in-law and innumerable aunts, uncles and cousins. That, church and a few close friends was about all he could manage, frankly.

As he drove toward his old apartment building, a feeling of déjà vu overcame him. He remembered well the day, almost a decade ago, when he'd first moved into the small, bland efficiency apartment. A heady feeling of liberation had suffused him then. He'd felt so proud to have left the home of his parents and struck out on his own, leaving behind two pesky younger sisters and two nosy older ones.

Of course, with more freedom had come greater re-sponsibility. Then had come the hard-won understand-ing that responsibility itself could be counted even more of a joy than any foolish, youthful notions of "free-dom" that he'd once entertained. A fellow could take pride in meeting his responsibilities and meeting them well, whereas freedom—as he had learned—could be-come an empty exercise in keeping loneliness at bay.

Other lessons had followed. He'd found his best friends in moments of difficulty rather than fun, though that was important, too. Most significant, Vince had learned that those who truly loved him—his family, particularly his parents—were bulwarks of support rather than burdens of bondage. The mature Vince possessed a keen awareness that not everyone was as richly blessed in that area.

For the life he had built and the man he had become, he had his parents, with their thoughtful guidance, patience, loving support and Christian examples, to thank. For his parents, he could only thank God, which was not to say that from time to time they did not make him wish that he lived on a different continent, particularly when it came to his single status.

By the time he pulled into the rutted parking lot of the small, dated, two-story apartment building, Vince was feeling pretty mellow with memories. He was by nature a fairly easygoing type, but he possessed a certain intensity, too, an innate drive that had served him well in building his business. Looking around the old place as he left the vehicle and moved onto the walkway, he saw that nothing whatsoever had changed, only his circumstances.

Onward and upward, he mused, setting foot on the bottom step of an all-too-familiar flight of stairs. His heavy, steel-toed boots rang hollowly against the open metal treads as he climbed. After passing three doors on the open landing, he stopped at the fourth and automatically reached for the doorknob. Only at the last moment did he derail his hand, lifting it and coiling it into a fist. Before his knuckles could make contact with the beige-painted wood, however, the door abruptly opened and a feminine face appeared. Obviously she had heard him coming.

"Who are you?"

Vince looked down into clear green eyes like pale

jade marbles fringed with sandy-brown lashes. Large and almond-shaped, they literally challenged him. He backed up a step, lowering his hand and took in the whole of her oval face.

It was a bit too long to be labeled classically pretty, just as her nose seemed a bit too prominent to be called pert. But those eyes and the lush contours of a generous mouth, along with high, prominent cheek-bones and the sultry sweep of eyebrows a shade darker than her golden-brown hair made a very strik-ing, very feminine picture, indeed. The hair was the finishing touch, her "crowning glory," as the Scrip-tures said. Thick and straight with a healthy, satiny shine, it hung well past her shoulders, almost to her elbows.

Vince suddenly had the awful feeling that his mouth might be agape. He cleared his throat, making sure that it wasn't, and finally registered her question.

"I'm, uh, Vincent Cutler. You left a message on my—"

"Well, it's about time!" she exclaimed, sweeping her wispy bangs off her forehead with one hand and then instantly brushing them down again. "I've got a whole bag full of your mail here. You must be on every mail-ing list in the country."

He nodded in thoughtless agreement, but she whirled away too abruptly to notice. He watched the agitated sway of her hips as her long legs carried her across the floor. She moved toward the narrow counter that sepa-rated the tiny corner kitchen from the rest of the single room and he instinctively followed.

"I tried dropping it off at the post office," she com-plained, "but they just kept sending it right back to me.

Doesn't matter that it hasn't got my name on it. It's got my address. That's all they care about apparently."

"Guess so," Vince mumbled, shrugging.

A raised ten-by-ten-foot platform set off by banisters denoted the sleeping area, and the remaining floor space served as dining and living rooms. A small bathroom containing a decent-sized closet opened off the latter. He knew all this without bothering to look, the apartment being as familiar to him as his own face in a mirror. Besides, his attention was fully taken by the tall, slender, feminine form in worn jeans and a simple, faded T-shirt, mostly obscured by the fall of her hair.

When she bent to open a cabinet door and reach inside, gentlemanly impulse sent his gaze skittering reluctantly around the room. Color jolted him as his eyes took in a bright-yellow wall and a neat, simple plaid of yellow, red and green against a stark white background. Potted plants were scattered about, and he registered a smattering of tiny checks and a few ruffles, but the room was not overly feminine as his mother's and sisters' houses were inclined to be. The furnishings were sparse and dated, obviously used, but the overall effect was surprisingly pleasing, much better than the drab, often cluttered place that he had inhabited.

"Wow," he said, and the next thing he knew, she was flying at him, both hands raised.

"What are you doing? Get out! Get out!"

She hit him full force, palms flat against his chest, propelling him backward. Vince threw his arms out in an attempt to regain his balance and then felt them knocked down again as he stumbled backward through the door, which summarily slammed in his face, just inches from his nose. Automatically reaching up, he checked to be certain that it hadn't taken a blow and felt the small familiar hump of a previous break. That was when he heard the bolt click and the safety chain slide into place.

For another moment, he was too stunned even to think, but then he began to replay the last few minutes in his mind, and gradually realization came to him. He slapped both hands to his cheeks. Good grief! She hadn't invited him in; he'd just followed her like some lost puppy, right into her home! *Her* home, *not* his, not any longer. No wonder she'd freaked! He dropped his hands.

"Oh, hey," he said to the door, feeling more and more like an idiot. "I—I didn't mean to alarm you. I would never…that is, I—I used to live here," he finished lamely.

She, of course, said nothing.

He closed his eyes, muttering, "Way to go, Cutler. Way to go. Probably scared the daylights out of her."

Shifting closer, he tried to pitch his voice through the door without really raising it; he knew too well how thin the walls were around here. "I'm sorry if I frightened you."

He waited several seconds, but there might have been a brick wall behind that door rather than a living, breathing woman. Actually, he had no idea if she was even still in the vicinity. She might have been cowering in the farthest corner of the room, though he couldn't quite picture her doing so.

No, a woman like that wouldn't be cowering. More likely she was standing there with a baseball bat ready to bash in his head if he so much as turned the doorknob. Clearly, a prudent man would retreat.

Despite recent evidence, Vince Cutler was a prudent man.

He turned and walked swiftly along the landing, then quickly took the stairs and swung around the end of the railing toward his truck. A certain amount of embarrassment mixed with chagrin dogged him as he once more climbed behind the wheel, his errand an obvious bust. Yet, a smile kept tweaking the corners of his mouth as he thought about the woman upstairs.

She was all dark gold, that woman, dark gold and vinegar. Spunky, that's what she was. He recalled that the top of her head had come right to the tip of his nose. Considering that he stood an even six feet in his socks, she had to be five-seven or eight, which would explain those long legs. It occurred to him suddenly that he didn't even know her name; that, more than anything else, just seemed all wrong.

As he turned the big truck back onto the street, he also turned his mind to mending fences. She still had his mail, after all, and he couldn't let things lie as they were. Good manners, if nothing else, decreed it. The question was how to approach her again. Frowning, he immediately sought solutions in the only manner he knew.

"Lord, I don't know what happened to my good sense. I scared that girl. Please don't let her sit there afraid that I'd hurt her. The whole thing was my fault, and if You'll just show me how, I'll try to make up for it."

Just then he drove by a minivan with the tailgate raised. It was parked in an empty lot and surrounded by hand-lettered signs touting Tyler roses, buckets of which were sitting on its back deck. A strange, unexpected thought popped into his head, one so foreign and seemingly out of nowhere that it startled him, and then he began to laugh.

That's what happened when you relied on God to

lead you. As his daddy would say, when you ask God for guidance, you'd better get out of the way quick. Now all he had to do was pick his time and his words very carefully. That was to say, very prayerfully.

Vince polished the toe of one boot on the back of the opposite pants leg, not a work boot this time but full-quill ostrich, one half of his best pair of cowboy boots. Armed to the teeth with two dozen bright red rosebuds, he took a deep breath, squared his shoulders and rapped sharply on the door. He counted to six before the door opened this time.

Green eyes flew wide, but he thrust flowers and words at her before he could find himself facing that door again. "I'm so sorry. I didn't meant to frighten you or seem disrespectful." When she didn't immediately slam the door in his face, he hurried on. "I guess I just lived here so long that it seemed perfectly natural to walk inside. I didn't think how inappropriate it was or how it would seem to you." She frowned and folded her arms, giving her head a leonine toss. He found himself smiling. "Honest. I feel like a dunce."

"You're grinning like one," she retorted, and then she sniffed.

His smile died, not because she'd insulted him—he didn't take that seriously—but because she'd obviously been crying.

"Oh, hey," he said, feeling like a real heel. "You okay?"

She swiped jerkily at her eyes and lifted her chin. "Yeah, sure I'm okay. You going to beat me with those flowers or what?"

"Huh?" He dropped his arm then quickly lifted it again, saying, "These are for you."

One corner of her mouth quirked, and humor suddenly glinted in those clear green eyes. "Yeah, I figured."

"For, uh, your trouble." He shifted uncertainly. "The mail and all."

"And all?" she echoed, arching one brow.

He gave her his most charming smile and waggled the roses in their clear plastic cone. "I said I was sorry."

She reached out and languidly swept the flowers from his grasp, drawling, "Right. Thanks. I suppose you want your mail now."

He nodded and fished a folded card out of his pocket, offering it to her. "I've already turned in one, but I thought you might want to drop that in the box yourself, so you'll know for sure that it's done."

She glanced at the change-of-address card, and that brow went up again. "That's you? Cutler Automotive?"

Nodding, he dipped into the hip pocket of his dark jeans and came up with a couple of coupons. "That reminds me. Maybe you can use these sometime."

She tucked the change-of-address card into the roses and took these new papers into one hand, cocking her head to get a good look at them.

"Hmm," she said, reading the top one aloud, "Fifty percent off service and repairs." She looked him right in the eye. "This on the up-and-up?"

"Absolutely."

"No catch? I don't have to spend a certain amount or agree to some extra service?"

"Nope. You just present the signed coupon, we knock fifty percent off your bill."

"No strings attached?"

"We don't accept photocopies," he pointed out, calling her attention to the smaller print at the bottom of the paper. "But that's it."

She nodded, apparently satisfied. "Okay. Great. If you wait right here, I'll get your mail."

"These feet are not moving," he promised, but the instant she turned her back, he craned his neck to get another look around.

She'd done wonders with the old place. Despite the dated furniture and faded fabrics, the apartment had a homey, put-together feel about it that he quite liked, and he told her so.

"Never looked this good when I lived here."

She laid the flowers on the counter and turned to face him. "No?"

He shook his head and shrugged. "Guess I just don't have the knack."

"What guy does?"

"None I know of, not many women, either, from what I can tell."

"You pay attention to that sort of thing, do you?" she asked, seeming surprised. It had sounded a little odd, now that he thought about it.

"Lately, I do. Since the move."

"Ah."

She bent and extracted a small shopping bag from the cabinet.

"This is it," she said, carrying the bag toward him. "Two more pieces came just today."

He reached through the open doorway to accept the bag. It was stuffed with papers.

"I'm sorry about this. I usually take better care of business."

"I just hope there aren't any overdue bills in there," she said dryly.

"Naw, I try not to have any of those."

"We all try," she quipped wryly, but he detected a troubled note.

"Not all," he said, wanting to reassure her somehow. "You'd be surprised how many people make no attempt to pay their bills."

"Maybe they can't."

"Maybe," he admitted, "but if they try, we work with them."

She tilted her head and her brows bounced up and down at that. "Cutler Automotive, you mean."

"Yes, ma'am."

"Huh."

After a second or two it became apparent that she wasn't going to say anything else, and he couldn't for the life of him think of any way to rectify that. He shuffled his feet in place.

"Well, you have a nice evening."

She reached for the door. "Yeah, you, too, if you can with all that to go through." She nodded at the sack in his arms. "If any more comes, I'll send it on your way now that I have a good address."

"I don't mind coming after it again," he assured her quickly, "if you'll just call."

"I'll send it," she stated decisively.

Defeated, he nodded. "Okay. However you want to handle it."

"That's how I want to handle it," she said flatly, backing up to push the door closed. "So long, Vincent Cutler."

He put up a hand. "Wait a sec. I'd like to know your

name, at least. I mean, if you don't mind." He shrugged. "Seems strange bringing flowers to a woman whose name I don't even know."

She considered a moment longer then said, "Jolie."

"Jo Lee," he repeated carefully.

"No." She rolled her eyes. "Jolie. J-o-l-i-e."

"Ah. That's pretty. Jolie what?"

She flattened her mouth, but then she answered. "Jolie Wheeler. Jolie Kay Wheeler."

He smiled again for some reason. It just sounded…right. "Jolie Kay. I'll remember that."

"If you say so."

His smile stretched into a grin. "Good night, Jolie Kay Wheeler. Maybe I'll see you around."

"I doubt it."

He didn't. He didn't know why, but even as that door closed to him once again, he knew somehow that he hadn't seen the last of spunky, pretty Jolie Wheeler. Strangely enough, that thought was quite all right by him.

Jolie reached into the cabinet overhead and brought down a big pickle jar to serve as a vase. After filling it with tap water, she turned to the counter where the tightly budded roses waited. No one had ever brought her flowers before. Figured it would be some goofball like Cutler. First he doesn't bother to have his mail forwarded, and then he strolls right in as if he owns the place, as if an open door is an automatic invitation to invade the premises.

The good-looking ones were always like that, thought they had a right to the whole world just because they were easy on the eyes. He was easier than most, with that pitch-black hair, lazy, blue-gray eyes, square jaw and dimples. More polite than most, too.

He had immediately apologized yesterday for invading her space, but her heart had been slamming against her rib cage so violently that she hadn't found enough air to reply. Then embarrassment had taken over, and she'd mulishly let him stand there and wheedle until he'd given up and gone away.

Actually, he seemed harmless enough. Now.

The day before when she'd looked up and found him standing there in the middle of her apartment as if sizing up the joint, he'd appeared eight feet tall and hulking. Today, of course, he'd been his usual six-foot—or thereabout—self. She hadn't imagined those broad shoulders and bulging biceps, though, or the slim hips and long legs. The truth was, she had panicked, which wasn't like her, but then she didn't know what she was like anymore. Nothing was as it had been. Without Russell.

She pushed away thoughts of her nephew, rapidly blinking against a fresh onslaught of tears.

This was getting to be a habit. She'd be okay for a while, and then something would remind her of that sweet baby face, that milky, gap-toothed smile and little hands that grasped so trustingly, coiling themselves in her hair and shirt. The loss still devastated her. More, it made her angry, at herself as much as at her sister and brother.

She should never have let herself love little Russ so completely. She should have treated him as nothing more than a foster child, his presence in her life temporary at best. After all, she knew only too well how the game was played. Ten years of experience on one side of that equation should have prepared her better for the other.

Oh, she had been placed with foster families who had truly tried to make her feel a part of the group, but she had always known that it would end. Something would happen, and she would be on her way again, shuffling from one home to another with heart-numbing regularity.

Somehow, though, she hadn't let herself think that it could happen with Russell. When Connie had first gone to prison, pregnant and unwed, she had talked about giving up her child for adoption. Then, after his birth, when she'd asked Jolie to take him and give him a good home, saying that he ought to be with family, Jolie had seen her opportunity to really have someone of her own.

She and Connie had never discussed what would happen after Connie got out. For one thing, Jolie had never dreamed that a judge would actually hand over the child whom she had raised as her own to her misguided younger sister, no matter that said sister had given birth to him. It wasn't fair, and to have their adored big brother Marcus side with Connie had been the unkindest cut of all.

Jolie was still grieving, but she supposed that was to be expected. It had only been days since she'd last seen him, eleven days, two hours, in fact. She could know how many minutes if she was foolish enough to check her watch, which she wasn't. Of course she was still grieving. She'd grieved her mother's absence for years, until she'd found out that Velma Wheeler was dead. Strangely enough, knowing that her mother had died was easier than believing that her mother had simply abandoned her children to the uncertain kindness of strangers.

Jolie shook her head and willed away the tears that had spilled from her eyes, telling herself that she would get on top of this latest loss. She'd had lots of practice.

Reaching for the roses, she slid them from their plastic cone and began arranging them in their makeshift vase. She did not realize, as the pleasing design began to take shape, that she made it happen with an innate, God-given ability which those lacking it would surely treasure.

Never once in her entire life had she ever imagined that anyone could admire or envy anything about her.

Chapter Two

Jolie picked up the two small rectangles of heavy paper from the counter top and studied them again, each in turn. One was the fifty-percent-off coupon that Vince Cutler had explained to her. The other promised a free tow. She wondered again what the catch might be, but she wasn't likely to find out until she had need of the services offered. And the need was very likely to arise.

Her old jalopy was a garage bill waiting to happen. The thing had been coughing and gasping like an emphysema patient lately. She'd literally held her breath all the way to work this morning.

If the dry cleaners where she was employed had been situated just a little closer to the new apartment, she'd have walked it every day just to save wear and tear on the old donkey cart, but five miles coming and going on a daily basis was a bit more than she could manage, especially with the evening temperatures hovering in the thirties. Just to be on the safe side, Jolie tucked the coupons into her wallet—never know when they might come in handy—before going back to the ironing with which she augmented her meager income.

Since the death of his wife, Mr. Geopp, owner and operator of the small, independent dry cleaners where she'd worked for the past six years, had chosen to outsource the delicate work rather than invest in the new machines that could handle it properly, and he'd stopped taking in alterations and regular laundry altogether.

One day, Jolie mused, Geopp would retire, and then what would she do? Her heart wasn't exactly in dry cleaning, but she didn't seem to possess a single exploitable talent. It was a familiar worry that she routinely shoved aside.

With the tip of one finger, she checked the temperature of the pressing plate, judged it sufficiently cooled not to damage the delicate silk blouse positioned on the padded board and carefully began removing the wrinkles from the fabric. Her mind wandered back to the coupons.

If she took in her car for an estimate, would she see Vince Cutler again?

She glanced ruefully at the flowers he had given her. They were a pretty pathetic sight now. The buds had opened and half the petals had fallen, but she couldn't bring herself to toss them just yet. Not that she was harboring any secret romantic fantasies about Vincent Cutler. She wasn't in the market, no matter how good-looking he was, and he was plenty good-looking. Why, the only thing that saved the man from being downright beautiful was the little hump on the bridge of his nose.

She couldn't help wondering how his nose had been broken, then she scolded herself for even thinking about him. Vince Cutler was nothing to her, and she intended to keep it that way. Secondhand experience had taught Jolie that romantic entanglements were more trouble than they were worth.

Her mom had been big on romance, and all that had gotten her was three kids by three different men, none of whom they could even remember. Still, every time some yahoo had crooked his finger at Velma Wheeler she'd followed him off on whatever wild escapade he'd proposed, often leaving her children to fend for themselves until she returned.

Sometimes they were out of food and living in the dark with the utilities shut off when she'd finally remember that she had a family. One day she simply hadn't returned at all, and eventually Child Welfare had stepped in to cart Jolie and her siblings off to foster care.

For years Jolie had harbored the secret fantasy that her mother would come back a changed woman, determined to reunite their scattered family, all the while knowing that Velma would have had to learn to care for them a great deal more in her absence than she ever had while present. Then one day Jolie had been told that her mother had died in a drunk-driving accident and been buried in a pauper's grave somewhere in Nevada. A simple typographical error had resulted in the misspelling of her name and an incorrect filing of records. Her mother had been gone four years by that time.

With Velma as their lesson, Jolie and her sister Connie had sworn that they would not go from man to man. Then Connie had somehow settled on that jerk Kennard and doggedly refused to give up on him. Jolie understood that Connie had feared being a serial loser just like their mom, but only after Kennard had gone to prison for the rest of his life, taking a pregnant Connie along with him, did she turn away from him. Of course, Connie had claimed that she hadn't even known that an armed robbery was being committed that day, let alone a murder, despite the fact that she had been sitting in front of the bank in a running car.

Jolie had been inclined to believe Connie at the time. Now she just didn't know.

Maybe if Connie had made a better choice than Kennard...but then, Jolie reminded herself, she wouldn't have had Russell. It was worth any hardship to have a little boy like that. Wasn't it?

Jolie shook her head. Thinking that way could get a girl in trouble. Better just to go it alone.

Jolie had learned that lesson the hard way after the authorities had split up her and her siblings when sending them into foster care. At first she and Connie had been placed together, but that hadn't lasted for very long.

Oh, they'd maintained contact. The department was good about that sort of thing. But the years had taken their toll. Jolie had been nine, Marcus only a year older and Connie just seven when their mom had disappeared.

Two decades later, Jolie was again alone.

With Russell to fill her days and nights and heart, it had seemed that she had family again, but only for a little while. Now all she had was a pile of other people's clothing to iron and a single room with a private bath to call her own—so long as she could pay the rent.

That thought sent her back to the job at hand, and for a time she lost herself in the careful placement and smoothing of one garment after another. Funny how you could take pride in something so small and insignificant as smoothing wrinkled cloth, but a girl had to get her satisfaction where she could.

"Come on, baby, just a little farther."

Jolie patted the cracked black dash encouragingly, but the little car sputtered and wheezed with alarming defiance. Then it gave a final paroxysm of shudders and simply stopped, right in the middle of rush-hour traffic.

"Blast!"

Someone behind her did just that with a car horn.

"All right, already!" she yelled, strong-arming the steering wheel as far to the right as she could. The car came to a rolling halt against the curb.

Tires screeched behind her. Another horn honked, and then an engine gunned. A pickup truck flew by with just inches to spare. Jolie flinched, put the transmission in Neutral and cranked the starter, begging for a break. The engine turned over, coughed and died again. The second time, the engine barely rumbled, and on the third it didn't do that much. By the fifth or sixth try, the starter clicked to let her know that it was getting the message but that the engine was ignoring its entreaties entirely. Jolie gave up, knowing that the next step was to get out and raise the hood.

She didn't dare try to exit the car on the driver's side. Instead, she turned on her hazard lights, put the standard transmission in first gear, set the parking brake and released her safety belt to climb across the narrow center console and the passenger seat to the other door. Stepping out on the grassy verge between the curb and the sidewalk, she tossed her ponytail off one shoulder and kicked the front wheel of the car in a fit of pique. Pain exploded in her big toe.

Biting her tongue, she limped around to the front end of the car to lift the hood and make her situation even more visible to the traffic passing on the busy street. After that, all she could do was plop down on the stiff brown grass to wait for someone to come along and offer to help as there was no place around from which to make a telephone call. Looked like she might be trying out those coupons from Cutler Automotive sooner rather than later. Provided someone with a telephone stopped.

More than half an hour had passed and her toe had stopped aching before a Fort Worth traffic cop pulled up behind her aged coupe, lights flashing. Traffic moved into the inside lane to accommodate him as he opened his door and got out. He strolled over to Jolie, a beefy African-American with one hand on his holster and the other on his night stick.

"Ma'am," he said pleasantly, "you can't leave your car here like this."

"Sir," Jolie replied with saccharine sweetness, "I can't get the thing to move."

He rubbed his chin and asked, "Anyone you can call?"

"Could if I had a phone."

He removed a cell phone from his belt and showed it to her. Heaving herself to her feet, she walked over to the car to take her wallet from the center console. Pulling out the coupon from Cutler Automotive, she handed it to him. Nodding, he punched in the number and passed her the phone.

The number rang just twice before a voice answered.

"Cutler Automotive. This is Vince. How can I help you?"

Vince. She swallowed and shifted her weight. "This is Jolie Wheeler."

"Well, hello, Jolie Wheeler. Have you got mail for me?"

"Nope. I've got a coupon for a free tow."

"A free tow?"

"That's what it says. Any problem with that?"

"No, ma'am. Where are you?"

She told him, and he said he'd be right there before hanging up. She handed the phone back to the officer and thanked him. He nodded and turned to watch the passing traffic, trying to make small talk. They'd covered how the car had been acting and where she was going and where she'd been and the state of disrepair of the Fort Worth streets by the time the white wrecker, lights flashing, swung to the curb in front of her crippled car.

Vince bailed out with hardly a pause, and Jolie's heart did a strange little kick inside her chest. Then he walked straight to the grinning cop, ignoring her completely.

"Jacob," he said, shaking the other man's hand.

The policeman smiled broadly and clapped Vince on the shoulder. "How you doing, my man?"

"Staying busy. How're you?"

"Likewise, only with very little sleep."

"New baby keeping you up nights?" Vince asked, flashing his dimples.

It was at this point that Jolie folded her arms, feeling very much on the outside looking in.

"Oh, man, is he ever!" came the ardent reply. "Rascal's got a set of lungs on him, too, let me tell you."

"Well, he sure didn't get those from his soft-spoken mama," Vince said with a grin.

"Soft-spoken?" Jacob the cop echoed disbelievingly. "Soft-spoken? My Callie? Man, you know better than that. You've sat in front of her at a football game."

Vince just grinned wider. "I'm going to tell her you said that."

"Not unless you want to attend my funeral." Both men laughed and back-slapped each other before Jacob moved off toward his patrol car. "You're in good hands now, ma'am," he called jovially to Jolie as he sauntered back to his vehicle.

Vince shook his head, still chuckling, and parked his hands at his waist, striking a nonchalant pose before finally turning to Jolie.

"Well, I'm glad you got a nice visit out of this," she said sarcastically.

Vince Cutler arched his brows, but his smile stayed firmly in place. "Jacob and I attend the same church, but because of his schedule we don't often get to the same service, so I'm glad to have seen him. Now, what's the problem with your car?"

She threw up her hands, disliking the fact that he'd made her feel glad, jealous and petty all in the space of a few minutes.

"How would I know? The hateful thing quit, that's all."

"Uh-huh." He stepped up to the bumper and looked over the engine. Gingerly, he wiped a forefinger across one surface and rubbed it against his thumb. "No oily emission."

"Is that good?" she asked anxiously, her concern about her transportation momentarily overcoming all else.

"It's not bad."

Whatever that meant.

She flattened her lips and tried to see what he saw as he leaned forward and fingered first one part and then another, poking and prodding at hoses and wires and other unnameable organs. Finally he turned to lean a hip against the fender.

"So what happened, exactly, before it quit running?"

She pushed a hand through her bangs, tugged at her ponytail and sucked in a deep breath, trying to remember *exactly.* Finally she began to talk about how the car had been coughing and sputtering by fits and starts lately and how the dash lights had blinked off from time to time.

He listened with obvious attention, then asked, "Any backfiring?"

She considered. "No, I don't think so."

"Okay." Pushing away from the car, he moved toward the driver's door. "Keys in the ignition?"

"Yes."

He opened the door and folded himself into the seat behind the wheel. The starter clicked for several seconds then stopped.

Vince spent a few moments looking at the gauges on the dashboard, then he got out and walked back to the wrecker, returning quickly with a small tool box and a thick, quilted cloth, which he spread on the fender before placing the tool box atop it. He opened the box and extracted a strange gizmo that resembled a calculator with wires attached, which he carried back into the car with him.

Jolie walked around to the passenger window and looked in while he wedged himself under the dash and began pulling down wires. He separated several little plastic clips and attached leads from the gizmo to them, then he studied the tiny screen before turning the ignition key on and off several times in rapid succession.

"What is that thing?" Jolie asked, curiosity getting the better of her.

"I call it my truth-teller."

"Oh, they sell truth at mechanic's school, do they?"

"They sure do," he drawled, ignoring her sarcastic tone.

"That's not what I heard."

"You heard wrong, then."

He removed the leads, reconnected the clips and tucked everything back up under the dash. Then he rose and carried his equipment around to the front of the car again. Jolie joined him there, more curious than ever. He didn't keep her waiting.

"You've got a sensor going out, and I'd guess that the alternator needs to be rebuilt, too."

Dismay slammed through her. She covered it by rolling her eyes. "And what's that going to cost?"

He shrugged. "Can't say without checking a parts list."

"More than a hundred?"

"Oh, yeah. Plus, you've got half a dozen hoses ready to spring leaks and at least one cracked battery mount that I can see. That'll have to be replaced before your next inspection. And if I were you, I'd have the timing chain checked."

She caught her breath, stomach roiling. How would she ever pay for all that? she wondered sickly.

"I've reset the sensor," he went on, "so it should behave for a little while, and I'll give you a jump to get you started, but you really ought to bring the car in soon as you can because this *will* happen again. Just a matter of time."

Jolie bit her lip. Maybe he was just shilling for the garage. Maybe this would be all it took. Whatever, she had zero intention of taking the car in for repairs until she had no other option. She folded her arms again as he went back to the wrecker and returned with what looked like a battery on wheels.

"How much is today going to cost?" she wanted to know, not that she had much choice at the moment.

"This? *Nada.*"

Jolie blinked. "Nothing?"

"I can charge you if you want," he said, mouth quirking at the corners.

She wrinkled her nose. "Thanks, but no thanks."

He smiled knowingly, dimples wrinkling his lean cheeks. "Okay, then."

With that he got busy hooking up everything. Finally he got in and started her car. The engine fired right off and settled into its usual, uneven rumble. Jolie almost dropped with relief.

"Thank goodness."

He started disconnecting and packing away gear.

As he dropped the hood, she lost a short battle with herself and asked, "You won't get in trouble with your boss, will you? For not charging me, I mean."

Vince wiped his hands purposefully on a red cloth that he'd pulled from his hip pocket, holding her gaze.

"No problems there."

"You're sure?"

"Jolie, I *am* the boss."

She felt a tiny shock, but she'd practiced nonchalance so long that it came easily to her.

"Well, if you say so."

He folded the cloth and stuffed it back into his pocket with short, swift movements, saying, "Fact is, I own and operate three garages."

She blinked, impressed, but of course that would never do.

"All by yourself?" she quipped blandly.

He chuckled. "Not exactly. I have twenty-two employees, not counting the outsourcing, of course."

"Outsourcing," she echoed dully.

"Um-hm, bookkeeping, billing, that sort of thing."

"Ah."

And here she'd figured him for a regular joe. Just goes to show you, she thought, eying his dusky-blue uniform with reluctant new interest.

"If you call the shop tomorrow," he told her casually, "I can work you in." She lifted her eyebrows skeptically, and he went on, prodding ever so gently. "You really ought to have that work done."

Now she *knew* it was a scam. Soften up the mark with a little freebie, make her think you're as honest as the day is long, then get her in the shop and soak her good. Resetting that sensor was probably all the car had ever needed.

"We'll see."

"Okay," he said lightly. "Well, I'll be seeing you."

"Oh, really?" She tilted her head, studying him for signs of dishonesty. Had he somehow sabotaged her car so that she'd have to bring it to his shop?

He glanced away pointedly, his sculpted mouth thinning. "You know, not everyone in the automotive-repair business is a crook. In fact, despite our reputation for rip-offs, most mechanics are honest and highly trained."

To her absolute disgust, color stained her cheeks. "I didn't say you were a crook."

He just looked at her, his smoky-blue eyes flat as stone. "No, but you were thinking it."

Her chin rose defensively. "You have no idea what I was thinking."

"Don't I?"

He just stood there, staring at her, until she suddenly realized what he was waiting for. Her hauteur wilted in a pool of mortification. Still, she wasn't about to apologize.

"Okay, maybe I was thinking it, but you don't know how often someone like me gets ripped off."

"Someone like you?" he echoed uncertainly. "And what makes you so different from the rest of us?"

"I'm a single woman, for one thing."

His expression grew suspiciously bland. "I had noticed that."

"And I don't have a lot of money for another," she snapped, trying to offset the little thrill that his droll comment had produced.

"I would think that would make you less of a target for the unscrupulous, frankly," he said calmly.

Bitterly, she shook her head. "You would think wrong."

"I'm sorry to hear that."

She gulped at the sincere tone of his voice. "The thing is, I don't know enough about cars to guard against getting ripped off."

"You could learn," he suggested lightly. It sounded almost like an invitation.

She looked down at her toes. "I doubt that. I'm not the mechanical type."

"Just the suspicious type," he countered dryly.

Rolling her eyes up, she met his gaze. "I have reason to be."

"I wouldn't know about that," he said, his voice softening, "but I know this. You have nothing to fear from me, Jolie Kay Wheeler. On any score. Ever."

Now what could she say to that? Apparently he didn't expect a reply, for he started toward the wrecker.

"Well, you try to have a good evening."

"Yeah, you, too," she grumbled, disliking the mishmash of feelings that swamped her.

He flipped her a wave, climbed into the truck and drove off, leaving her standing there in the gathering twilight like some oversized, ponytailed traffic cone. Glancing around self-consciously, she made her way to the driver's seat of her little car and dropped down into it.

A sedan flew by with the blare of a horn. Traffic had moved back into the outside lane the instant Vince and his flashing lights had pulled away, but she had barely noted that fact. Shaking slightly, she switched on her headlamps, jammed the transmission into gear, put on her blinker, turned off her hazard lights and prepared to merge.

It hit her then. Like a ballpeen hammer to the back of the head.

She had never thanked him. A handsome, apparently successful man had gotten her car running for free, and she hadn't even had the grace to thank him properly. She tried to remember all the reasons why she had been right to suspect his motives, but somehow they didn't quite ring true.

Jolie brushed her bangs up, then down, blowing out

a stiff breath and closing her eyes until the world righted itself and equilibrium returned and she could look at the situation dispassionately.

On second thought, it just didn't figure. He had to have some ulterior motive, something so slick and cagey that she couldn't even think of it. And maybe— good gracious—maybe he was just a nice man who liked to help people. Stranger things had happened.

Somewhere.

Sometime.

Telling herself that it didn't matter, she took a last measuring look at traffic, then pulled away from the curb.

The problem was, somehow it did matter. A lot. Enough to make her feel small and petty and unreasonable.

She was halfway home before it occurred to her that she still had both of those coupons.

Vince shifted in his seat, the safety belt biting into his shoulder. He craned his neck, trying to work out a kink there. It was ridiculous, getting this worked up over a little thing like having his motives questioned. Everyone was suspicious of everybody, at least until they got to know one another. He'd been accused of having ulterior motives before, though not in quite some time. It wasn't pleasant, but it wasn't fatal.

So she didn't trust him. So what? The world was full of people who expected automotive repairmen to rip them off. It was foolish to think she would be any different. And what difference did it make, anyway? God had obviously brought her into his life so that he could get her old car running for her again, and that was just what he'd done. End of story.

The thing wasn't going to run for long, though. With just a cursory inspection he'd found enough wrong under that hood to keep him busy for days, but he'd only mentioned the worst of it because it was obvious that she didn't have much money. It was just as glaringly obvious that she wouldn't be easy to help, either.

Maybe that was the point.

If so, he'd definitely be seeing her again. He believed that God had a purpose in all that He allowed into the lives of His children. So if he never saw her again, so be it. It wasn't his business, after all, to second-guess God, and he was just fine with that.

So why was he fighting the urge to turn around and give her a lecture on the stupidity of looking a gift horse in the mouth?

Ridiculous. Just ridiculous.

He didn't know her well enough to be this disappointed in her attitude. And he probably never would. A hole seemed to open in his chest, burning hot around the edges.

Vince sighed and tried to concentrate on his driving. He passed an intersection on a green light and immediately heard the screech of tires followed at once by the crunching of metal. Automatically, Vince flipped on his warning lights and pulled out of traffic.

Looking around, he saw that two cars had collided in a grocery-store parking lot across the street. It didn't seem serious, and it wasn't impeding traffic, plus, he was off-duty. The fact was, he didn't make wrecker runs anymore. At least he hadn't until Jolie Wheeler had called. Well, that would teach him.

Shaking his head, he began making his way across the busy street to the parking lot. What was he going to do? Leave without making certain that no one needed his assistance? Not his style. Then again, neither was embarrassing himself, but he'd managed to do that twice now with Jolie Kay Wheeler. Twice was quite enough. Why couldn't he just leave well enough alone?

He reached the scene of the mishap, killed his engine and slid out onto the tarmac. Two women were glaring at each other over the hoods of their tangled cars. Vince put on a smile and waded into the fray.

"Can I help, ladies?"

Almost an hour later he'd managed to uncouple their bumpers and pull out a fender so both could be on their way, still angry but maintaining their civility even as they each contemplated a hike in insurance rates. Twenty bucks richer—the one with the crumpled fender had insisted on compensating him—Vince swung the wrecker through a fast-food lane to pick up a burger to eat at home. Alone.

He could've dropped in on his mom or one of the girls. They were always willing to set an extra plate at the table for him, but they were always wanting to know where he'd been and who he'd seen lately, too, and he just wasn't in the mood to answer questions about his nonexistent love life or hear how he worked too much. He wasn't in the mood to eat alone, either, but those were the options. With a sigh, he resigned himself to the latter.

It was only later as he bit into his burger at the kitchen counter that he wondered if Jolie would call on Cutler Automotive when her old jalopy finally conked on her again, because conk it would—and she still hadn't redeemed those coupons.

Feeling a little better, he enjoyed the rest of his burger.

Chapter Three

"Aaargh!"

Jolie smacked the steering wheel with a closed fist. Not again! This time the engine wouldn't even turn over. No cough, no sputter, nothing.

She'd have cried if it would've done any good, but tears wouldn't pay for automotive repairs. Air wouldn't either, and that's what was in her checking account at the moment, with payday still two days away and rent due next week.

To make matters worse, she was going to miss at least a few hours of work this morning. The week was not starting out well. Sick at heart, she wrenched her keys from the ignition and crawled out of her old four-banger—*no*-banger at the moment—to head back upstairs.

Her first telephone call was to Mr. Geopp, who told her only to get into work when she could. He was a pleasant enough employer but somewhat distant personally. His late wife had been easier to talk and relate to. She'd cut Jolie every possible break, especially after Russell had arrived.

Jolie would stay with Geopp for no other reason than loyalty to the memory of his wife. She just wished that he would display a little more emotion, if only to let her know for sure where she stood with him in moments like this. It was one more worry on a long list of worries.

Jolie sat down to think through her options with the car. It had started before with a simple jump from a battery charger. Maybe that would work once more. She judged her chances of getting it done for free a second time at slim to none, however, especially if she called Cutler's again. After questioning Vince's integrity, she doubted that he'd cut her a break. Then again, neither would any other emergency service in town.

She thought of the coupons and shook her head in resignation. Cutler Automotive probably jacked up the price twice as high as normal before giving their fifty percent discount, but at least the towing would be free. They couldn't jack up free.

Sighing, she reached for the telephone once more. This time a perky-sounding female answered the call.

The wrecker arrived twenty-four minutes later.

Jolie was sitting on the bumper tapping one toe against the pavement when the familiar white truck swung into the lot. Her stomach lurched in anticipation, but then a stranger opened the driver's door and got out.

"You Ms. Wheeler?"

Nodding, Jolie tamped down her disappointment and straightened away from the car to look over this newcomer.

He seemed roughly the same age as Vince and had a shock of very dark hair falling forward over his brow, but that was where the similarities ended. This fellow was shorter and wider than Vince with a noticeable bulge around the middle and a slight under-bite that made his lower jaw seem overlong. His brown eyes twinkled merrily as he thrust out his right hand.

"I'm Boyd. What can I do for you?"

"You can make my car go."

"Well, let's have a look," he said noncommitally, taking a toolbox from the truck, "and while I'm looking, why don't you tell me what's been going on with it?"

Jolie started with that morning's fiasco and worked her way backward over the past couple weeks, leaving out only Vince's diagnosis. By the time she was through with her tale, he was nodding his head knowingly.

"Sounds like the alternator and probably a bad sensor. I'll try resetting the sensor and jump-starting it."

Jolie breathed a sigh of relief, but it was for naught. The sensor would not register, according to Boyd, and the jump did no good.

"Well, I'll tow her in and see what a full diagnostic turns up," he said blandly.

"What's that going to cost?" Jolie asked, fishing the coupons from the hip pocket of her jeans. "I have these."

Boyd took the coupons, kept the one for the free tow and handed back the other, saying, "These'll help."

"So how much?"

He shrugged. "Provided it's what I think it is and we don't find any other problems, I'd say about three hundred, but a lot depends on the parts. This is a domestic car, but a lot of the parts are foreign-made, so…" He shrugged again.

Jolie felt physically ill.

"Is that three hundred before or after the discount?"

He looked at her sympathetically. "After."

She momentarily closed her eyes.

"I can't afford that!"

"Aw, don't worry," he told her. "The boss will cut you a deal."

That would be the boss whom she'd practically called a crook.

"I wouldn't count on it," she muttered.

Boyd chuckled. "No, really. Vince is a good guy. He helps people out all the time. Between you and me, he'd probably give the business away bit by bit if I didn't keep reminding him that he was supposed to be making a profit. But then, the way I figure it, God takes care of His own."

Jolie didn't know about that. She just knew that life had suddenly gotten immeasurably more difficult for her personally, and it hadn't exactly been a walk in the park to begin with.

"I don't know how I'm going to manage this."

"Listen, just call the shop later and speak to Vince," Boyd urged. "Use the second number on the coupon. Okay?"

"Sure."

The two of them were probably working the scam together, she thought sullenly, and the nice-guy acts were just a carefully coordinated part of it.

Then again, the car wasn't faking it. The thing had been bugging out on her since well before Vincent Cutler had showed up on the scene.

Boyd had her put the car in Neutral so he could push it out of its parking space and "get a good hook on it." A few minutes were all that were required to secure the towing device. Then he just started up the automatic winch, and they stood there watching the front end of her car slowly rise off the ground.

"I have to find a ride to work," Jolie muttered to herself.

"Yeah? Where do you work?"

She told him, and he jerked his head toward the cab of the truck. "Get in. I'll drop you."

She brightened. That was the first bit of good news she'd had today.

"Really?"

"It's on the way."

"Great."

She climbed into the cab of the truck while he finished securing the tow. It was spotlessly clean, despite a gash in the vinyl of the bench seat, and sported a two-way radio, GPS system and some sort of miniature keyboard attached to the dash with an electronics cord.

As soon as Boyd slid beneath the steering wheel, he picked up the keyboard and typed in some letters and numbers, then he triggered the radio and informed whoever was on the other end that he was headed back to the garage with a car in tow, rattling off both make and model.

Soon Jolie was standing in front of the dry cleaners watching her car move away behind the wrecker, its front end pointing skyward. Mindlessly, she swept her bangs back and then smoothed them down again before turning to enter the shop. Bumping into one of their regular customers, she pasted on a smile. A glance showed her that the shop was full and the counter vacant while Geopp evidently searched for garments to be picked up. She went to work.

"How are you, Mrs. Wakeman?"

"Arthritis just gets worse and worse," came the usual doleful reply.

"That's too bad. How many pieces today?"

"Three, and be careful of the gold buttons on the blazer. They tarnished last time."

"Yes, ma'am."

The rest of the morning proved as busy as those first few minutes, but Jolie's mind was never far from her troubles.

Immediately after lunch, she called the garage, using the number on the card that Boyd had given her. Vince answered this time.

"Cutler Automotive. This is Vince speaking. How can I help you?"

She gulped inaudibly. "This is Jolie Wheeler again."

"Oh, hi. We've got the car on diagnostics now."

He sounded perfectly normal, as if she hadn't insulted him, as if they were friends or something equally ridiculous. For some reason that rankled, adding a dry edge to her voice.

"So you still don't know what's really wrong with it?"

"We don't have confirmation, no."

"And when will you have confirmation?"

"Shortly."

"Call me as soon as you know what it's going to cost," she demanded.

"All right."

"*Before* you do any work."

Several seconds of silence followed that, and when next he spoke, his voice was tinged with annoyance.

"No one's going to take advantage of you, Jolie."

She went on as if she hadn't heard him.

"Because I really can't afford a big repair bill." Or any repair bill for that matter.

He sighed gustily.

"I realize that. Look, why don't you just come by the shop after work? I'll show you exactly what's wrong with your car and what it's going to cost to fix it, and we'll figure out how to take care of it. Okay?"

He couldn't have sounded more reasonable, so why did she feel like needling him?

"And just how would you suggest I get over there without transportation? Take the bus?"

It was an entirely plausible possibility, which made what happened next all the more inexplicable.

"I'll pick you up," he said lightly. "What time to do you get off work?"

She didn't even balk, which in itself was appalling.

"Six o'clock."

"Okay. See you then."

They quickly got off the phone after that. Jolie stood staring at the thing for a long moment, wondering what on earth had possessed her to agree that he should pick her up, but then she shook her head.

Why shouldn't he? He had her car, after all. She hoped she could wangle a ride home out of it, too. Beyond that, she just refused to think, period.

Vince pulled up to the curb in front of the dry cleaners at precisely three minutes past six. The shop had obviously seen better days. Its storefront looked outdated and rather dingy, but the area was clean and safe. Because he was in a ten-minute loading zone, he kept the engine running and settled back to wait.

He didn't have to wait long. The door opened just

moments later, and Jolie burst out onto the sidewalk. He grinned at her dropped jaw. Her ragged little car was purring like a contented kitten.

"It's fixed!"

He laughed at her delight, but then her face turned thunderous. Her hands went to her hips, and he *knew* what she was going to say. Even as she spoke, he released his safety belt, opened the door and stood, one foot still inside the car, one hand on the steering wheel.

"I did *not* authorize any work."

"No, you didn't," he interrupted, "but it had to be done."

"You said we'd talk about it first!"

"Jolie, how would you get back and forth to work without your car?"

She put a hand to her head, ruffling her bangs and then smoothing them again. Vince tried not to smile at what seemed to be a characteristic gesture, something she did without conscious thought.

"I can't pay for it!" she suddenly wailed, as if he didn't know that.

The sidewalk was not the place to talk about it, however.

"Get in," he told her, indicating the passenger seat. For a moment she just stared at him. "Get in," he repeated. "My truck's back at the shop. We can talk on the way."

· She trudged around and got into the car with all the enthusiasm of a prisoner on the way to her execution. He chuckled despite his better judgment.

"It's not funny," she grumbled as he dropped down into the seat and clipped his belt once more.

"It's not tragic, either."

"Shows what you know," she snapped. "When was the last time you had to choose between paying the rent and other obligations?"

"It's been some while," he admitted, "but I have been there."

"Then you understand that there's just no way…" She gulped. "A—a few bucks a month, maybe, if I—"

"Will you just listen for a minute?" he urged, laying his arm along the back of her seat in entreaty.

She frowned at him, worry clouding those jade-green eyes.

"I have an idea about how we can square this."

Her mouth compressed suspiciously. It was a very pretty mouth, wide and mobile and full-lipped, but he couldn't help wondering what or who had fostered that mistrustful expression.

"How?" she asked.

He glanced at the front of the dry cleaners.

"Well, if it's not a conflict of interest for you, I need someone to do my laundry."

She blinked.

"Laundry?"

"Yeah, you know, dirty clothes and shop rags, some linens, that sort of thing."

The clouds were beginning to lift from her eyes, but her tone was tart as she retorted, "I know what laundry is, but why should I do yours?"

She buckled her safety belt, and Vince put the transmission in gear, turning away so that she wouldn't notice that he struggled with a sudden grin.

"Garages are dirty places," he began, nosing the car into traffic, "and I own all the uniforms that the guys wear. I thought I could do the washing myself, even bought a top-of-the-line, extra-capacity washer-and-dryer set, but it just doesn't get done in a timely manner."

"And you want to pay me to do it."

"Something like that."

She flipped the end of her ponytail off her shoulder, obviously thinking.

"I get it. You're talking about a barter arrangement, basically."

He nodded and signaled with the blinker that he was moving the car over into the next lane.

"Unless, like I said before, it's a conflict of interest for you, given that your regular job is with a dry cleaner."

"Not a problem. Mr. Geopp stopped taking in laundry a few months ago after his wife died."

"That's too bad, about his wife, I mean."

"Yeah, she was a good lady," Jolie said lightly, but something about her tone let him know that she honestly grieved the woman's passing.

"Were you friends?"

"Not really," Jolie replied, looking away. "About the laundry…"

He took the hint and dropped the subject.

"I have to warn you, there's lots of it."

"Good. That means I'll get the debt worked off sooner rather than later."

He nodded, signifying that they had come to an agreement in principle at least.

"Okay, so all we have to do is negotiate the particulars. I understand that laundry costs are figured by the pound or by the piece."

"That's right."

"I don't have any way to weigh it, so I say we go by the piece, then, if that's agreeable to you."

She named a price that was very much in line with what he'd expected, given that he would be providing the equipment and the necessary supplies. He proposed drawing up a debit sheet so she could mark off her work and subtract the cost of it from the repair bill, which would reflect the fifty-percent reduction that she'd been promised and that would include some extra repairs to her car that he felt were necessary but which he had not yet done.

"I only have two days a week to devote to this," she warned him.

"And what two days would those be?"

"Sunday and Monday. Those are my days off from the dry cleaners."

He shook his head.

"Sundays are for church. I'll be content with Mondays."

"No matter how long it takes for me to work off the debt?" she pressed.

"No matter how long it takes," he assured her.

She stared out the window for a long time, her expression hidden from him. He waited, confident of her decision. Finally she looked straight ahead.

"Okay, it's a deal."

He let her see his smile.

"Let me show you where you'll be working, then."

"Might as well." She sat up a little straighter.

"Obviously this street is Hulen," he pointed out, slowing to make a right turn. "We're going to take the Interstate up here and head west for about a mile."

She nodded, obviously making mental notes as he drove and talked her through the route.

When he turned the car down his street, she drew her brows together and said, "This can't be right."

"What do you mean? It's right up here."

"Here?" she echoed uncertainly, indicating the neighborhood around them with a wave of her hand.

The development was brand-new, not even half occupied yet, but that didn't explain her confusion to him. He let it go long enough to pass by the two empty lots between the corner house and his own at the top of the rise.

"This is it."

He couldn't help the note of pride in his voice.

By some standards, it was a modest home, but it was everything he had ever wanted, bright, roomy, well-appointed and undeniably attractive with its gabled metal roof and exterior of natural stone and rich red brick. He'd labored over every detail, probably to the point of driving the architect and builder nuts, but this was the place where he intended to live out the bulk of his life and, he hoped, one day raise a family.

Most folks didn't look at a first house as a long-term home, but Cutlers weren't the sort who "traded up." They were the kind of people who put down roots, sank them deep and let the years roll by in relative contentment. They believed in God, family, personal integrity, hard work and generosity, all notions that he'd once found boring and mundane. He'd gotten over all that, and he hadn't questioned his values again—until he saw the look on Jolie Wheeler's face as he turned her old car into his curving driveway.

She hated the place; he could see it on her face, and his gut wrenched. Disappointment honed a fine, defensive edge onto his voice.

"What's wrong with it?"

"What's wrong?" she echoed shrilly. "It's your house!"

"You expected me to take you to someone else's house?"

"I expected you to take me to your *business,* one of your garages!"

He stared at her, realization dawning.

"You thought I'd put a washer and dryer in one of my shops?"

"Of course I did!"

He stroked his chin, thinking. Guess he hadn't ever said that the appliances were at his house, and he *had* mentioned uniforms and shop rags and dirty garages.

"Never thought about putting a laundry room into the shop," he mumbled. "Might not be a bad idea. I'll have to look into that."

She threw up her hands, clearly exasperated.

"And in the meantime?"

He shrugged. "In the meantime we've got what we've got, don't we?"

She dropped her jaw, trying to see, apparently, just how far it could go without dislocating. He clamped his back teeth together and mentally counted to ten before drawing a calming breath and reaching way down deep for a reasonable tone.

"Look, I didn't mean to mislead you. The thought of putting a laundry room in the shop itself never even occurred to me."

"And you assumed that I understood you were taking me to your house?"

"Yeah, actually, I did."

She rolled her eyes at that.

"If you prefer," he offered grimly, "you can take the stuff to a commercial laundry somewhere."

"And who's going to pay for that?" she demanded.

"I will," he gritted out, hanging onto the wispy tail end of his patience, "but first you really ought to take a look at what my laundry room has to offer and what you'll have to haul around town if you decide that you just can't stand working here."

She turned her head to stare out the passenger window, drumming her fingers on the armrest attached to the door. He didn't know what else to say, what she expected him to say now, so he just waited her out. After some time she abruptly yanked the handle and popped up out of the car. Vince breathed a sigh of relief. He didn't know if his relief stemmed from her cooperation or the possibility that her disapproval was not directed at his home after all.

He killed the engine as she moved around the car toward the walkway. He got out, tossed her car keys to her and followed her along the curving walk to the front door. He didn't usually go in this way, preferring to park in the garage at the side of the house and enter through the back hall and kitchen, but he'd always admired the professional landscaping. In the summertime the flower beds beneath the front windows would blaze with purple lantana. Now he looked at it all with an especially critical eye, wondering what she thought of it, though why he should care was beyond him.

To put it bluntly, the girl was a charity case, and as prickly as a cactus. What difference did it make whether or not she approved of his house? Or him, for that matter? And yet it did. He couldn't help wondering why, but when it came right down to it, he was almost afraid to know.

Chapter Four

Jolie tried not to be impressed by the sprawling structure sitting proudly atop the gentle hill, but that wasn't easy. It rose up gleaming and perfect, like something out of a storybook, with its rock and brick exterior and shining metal roof. The walkway underfoot was constructed of the same red brick and brown stone as the house and was flanked by billowing hillocks of greenery and clumps of a spiky plant that looked like a big, spiny artichoke to her. She didn't know one plant from another, but she knew money on the ground when she saw it.

She couldn't wait to see the inside of the place, even if the hair had stood up on the back of her neck when she'd first realized where he'd brought her.

His house, for pity's sake!

What'd he think, that she would be so impressed she'd just fall all over him?

Not likely. No way. Uh-uh. She had better sense than that, thank you very much.

But, oh man, what a place.

Vince slipped past her on the brick porch, which was deeply inset beneath a tall arch, and jammed a key into the lock, giving it a quick twist. The tall, honey-colored wood plank door, inlaid with artistically rusted nail-heads and iron bands, swung open soundlessly, revealing stone floors and smooth walls plastered in pinkish-tan adobe. The tall narrow windows flanking the door were made of stained glass depicting two spiny cacti in a delicate green with blossoms of rose red.

He stepped back to let her pass, and she'd have wiped her feet before entering if there had been a mat of any sort. As it was, she wiped her hands surreptitiously on the seat of her worn jeans, just in case they were dirty, then tugged on the hem of her T-shirt to cover the self-conscious action. She tilted her head back in the foyer, looking up at least twenty feet to the ceiling, past an elegantly rustic wrought-iron chandelier with cut-glass shades.

To her left was a hallway. To her right stretched a huge room set off by tall arches. It was completely empty except for a pair of light fixtures, larger versions of the one hanging over her head, and a leafy fern that sat on the floor in front of a window covered by a faded bed sheet. Straight ahead Jolie spied the back of a nondescript sofa and the overhang of a bar topped in polished granite.

"This way," he said, leading her through the foyer and into what was obviously a den.

The sofa sat in front of a massive stone fireplace. Flanking the fireplace was an equally massive built-in unit which could easily contain a television set as large as a dining table. Upon it were a small framed photo of several kids with mischievous grins and a pile of paperback books. The only other furnishings in the room were a low, battered table and a utilitarian floor lamp. At least here the windows were covered with expensive pleated shades in a dark red.

The bar, she saw, opened onto a large kitchen, as did the arched doorways on each end. Louvered, bat-wing doors stood open to reveal an island containing a deep stone sink. Behind it rose enough cabinets to stash away all the cookware usually offered for sale in a small department store.

The brushed-steel fronts of the appliances announced that no expense had been spared in outfitting the space, but the countertops were bare except for a small toaster and a coffeemaker. At the end of the kitchen, surrounded by oriel windows and two doors, one that opened to a hallway and another leading outside, was a dining area large enough to dwarf the small round table and two chairs situated beneath another unique light fixture.

"Who lives here?" she wanted to know.

"I do."

She rolled her eyes at him. "Besides you."

"No one."

Bringing her hands to her hips, she stared at him in disbelief.

"You've got how many bedrooms in this place, two, three?"

"Four, actually."

"And you live here all by yourself?"

"That's right."

She looked around her, dumbfounded.

"It's a little bare," he said sheepishly, and that was putting it mildly. "I really need to get somebody in here to help me do it up right. Just can't figure out who."

Good golly, Miss Molly, what she could do with a place like this!

She couldn't imagine living here, but it was practically empty, almost a blank slate, and she could see just what ought to go where, starting with a pair of big, leather-upholstered, wrought-iron bar stools so company could sit there at the counter enjoying a cold drink while the host prepared dinner. And that island just begged for a big old pot rack, something sturdy and solid, not that the place lacked storage.

"Hire a decorator," she told him. Obviously he could afford professional help.

He wrinkled his nose at that. "I don't know. I'm not much for trends and themes. It's not a showroom, after all, it's a home."

"But the right decorator could do wonders in here," she insisted.

"Yeah, but who is the right decorator?" he asked rhetorically. He then effectively closed the subject by lifting a hand and saying, "Laundry room's this way."

He led her through the kitchen and into the hallway. After pointing out that the garage lay to the left, he turned right. The second door opened into a laundry room large enough to sport not only a top-of-the-line, front-loading washer-and-dryer set but also a pair of roll-away racks for hanging clothes, a work table for folding and an ironing board, plus a sink and various cabinets.

Dead center on the tiled floor lay a heap of clothing big enough to easily hide a full-grown man. Sitting up. Jolie's jaw dropped.

"How long have you been accumulating that?" she asked, pointing at the pile.

"Week, week and a half," he said mournfully. "By Friday there'll be about half that much again."

"Good grief!" she exclaimed, mentally rolling up her sleeves. "Looks like I've got my work cut out for me."

He lifted his hands. "So do I load it up or not?"

"In what?" she asked dryly. "You got a dump truck around here?"

He chuckled. "Not that I've noticed."

"Well, then," she said with a sigh, "I guess we'll do it your way."

He just grinned, blast his good-looking hide, and well he might. In his place she'd be grinning, too. She was smiling on the inside as it was. Working in a place like this was going to be an out-and-out pleasure, even if it was only temporary. If he tried anything funny with her, she'd just walk out and leave him and his laundry high and dry without the least qualm.

Looking at it that way, she couldn't lose, because whatever happened, her car would be fixed. She almost hoped he *did* try to take advantage of the situation, but not until her debt was paid off because she didn't like owing anybody anything.

Yes, sir, smiling on the inside.

For once, things were going to go her way.

"This one?" Jolie slowed the car as they drew near the corner. Vince shook his head.

"No, the next."

She sped up again, laughing when the little car responded with more pep than usual. "I can't get over how much better it runs."

"It'll drive even smoother with the tires rotated and

balanced," he told her. "You might notice a little improvement when we get all the hoses replaced, too, but probably not. You won't have to worry about another breakdown anytime soon, though."

"Music to my ears," she said, and he couldn't help smiling.

She drove as she seemed to do everything else, he noted, with an innate wariness. It certainly kept her on her toes and gave him some confidence in her safety on the road, but it also made him a little sad because she seemed to be constantly expecting trouble and catastrophe.

Over all, Jolie Wheeler struck him as a woman who'd had a lot of hard knocks in life, which was, he supposed, nothing new. The odd thing was that he didn't much like thinking of it.

The way she'd taken in his place had told him that she was unfamiliar with some of the more recent building trends. Later, she'd seemed to be mentally furnishing and decorating the space, and yet she'd remained oddly detached, admiring but certainly not gushing with compliments. He had sensed a kind of assumption on her part that she was out of her element in his house, and that had irritated him a little. Okay, a lot.

He was proud of his home. It was no mansion, but it was comfortable and spacious and extremely well-built. For the life of him, he didn't see why she shouldn't feel perfectly at ease in such surroundings, especially as he'd been particularly struck by how *right* the place felt for her. Maybe that accounted for the new idea noodling around in the back of his mind.

What he'd told her about needing help with furnishing and decorating the place was true. In fact it had begun to take on a certain urgency as his mother and sisters had started pressing him to let them have a go at it. He shuddered mentally, imagining what that might mean. If he wasn't very careful he'd walk into his own house one day soon and find it outfitted in chintz and lace and filled up with kitschy knickknacks.

He liked what Jolie had done with the apartment much more than what his mother and sisters had done with their respective homes. Could she be talked into giving him a hand with his place? He was trying to think how to broach the subject when his stomach gurgled and growled—more like roared, actually. It was so loud that Jolie burst out laughing.

Mildly embarrassed, he clapped a hand over his belly.

"Feeding time at the zoo, I take it," she teased.

"Hey, I'm a hardworking man, and it's dinnertime, okay?"

"Okay by me," she grinned.

Suddenly his heart was beating a little too pronouncedly as he made a spur-of-the-moment decision. He shifted in his seat, wondering if it was wise but knowing that he was going to do it. Fearing she could get the wrong idea, though, he made the suggestion as casually as he could manage.

"Listen, there's a pretty good restaurant up here on the right. Why don't we stop off and grab a bite?"

For a second, he got no reaction. Then she made a face, and he was sure that she was going to tell him to go soak his head. To his surprise, though, her answer was fairly ambiguous.

"I'm not really fit for going out after a day at the cleaners. It's dirty, smelly work, and—"

"You look good to me," he blurted and then could've bitten his tongue off—until she slipped him an almost hopeful glance out of the corner of her eye. "It's a casual sort of place," he added quickly. "I'm, uh, not exactly dressed for anything fancy, either." He indicated his uniform with a wave of one hand.

They came to a red light, and she gave him another one of those sideways looks.

"Just dinner," she said.

It could have been a question or a warning, but he decided to take it as the former, quipping, "Sure. You didn't think I was going to insist on going roller-skating afterward, did you?"

Her mouth quirked up in a smile.

"Do people still roller-skate? Isn't it all roller-blading now?"

He relaxed.

"Doggoned if I know. If you don't do it in a garage or on a field, I haven't had much experience with it."

They both chuckled and drove on in silence for a couple more blocks.

"That's it right up there," he said, and she turned off the street into the parking lot. "Best chicken-fried steaks in town," he told her as she parked.

After killing the engine she said dryly, "Let's hope there's something a little healthier on the menu."

"Well, sure," he teased, "they've got fried chicken, too."

She rolled her eyes as she climbed out of the car. Chuckling, he let himself out on the other side.

"The menu lists a bunch of salads," he assured her as they walked toward the restaurant. "I've even been known to eat one a time or two."

"I'll bet it had fried chicken on top of it," she retorted as he pulled open the door and held it for her.

So it had, but he let his grin be his admission, to her obvious amusement.

The hostess hurried toward them. A teenager in baggy cargo pants a size too large and a T-shirt a size too small, she wasn't dressed any better than they were. She greeted them with a smile and led them to a booth with bench seats and a plank table.

Vince ordered iced tea, chips and salsa as an appetizer and the chicken-fried steak for a main course. Jolie went for an Oriental salad with grilled chicken and mandarin oranges. They both asked for extra lemon with their tea.

Business seemed unusually slow, so the service was especially prompt, leaving them little time for talking. Even at that, he did most of it.

"So, Jolie Wheeler, tell me something about yourself."

She shrugged and said, "Not much to tell."

"What about your family?"

She looked down at the thick paper napkin in her lap. "Don't have much. What about you?"

"Too much." He chuckled and took it back. "Naw, not really. Thing is, I've got four sisters, and I'm smack dab in the middle."

"That must be trying at times."

"At times," he admitted. "The older two want to baby me all the time, and the younger two think their big brother is supposed to baby them. At least I got four brothers-in-law out of the deal."

"So they're all married then?"

"That's right, and they hate that I'm not. It's like their mission in life is to see that I am, theirs and Mom's."

"And why aren't you?" Jolie asked lightly.

He shrugged. "Haven't found the right lady yet."

"Oh, like you've been out searching high and low for her," she said, sounding very skeptical about that.

He rubbed his palms against his thighs and admitted, "Not lately. I'm open to it, though."

She seemed surprised by that.

The chips and salsa arrived then, and he was hungry enough to dive in, but from long habit, he bowed his head first and silently said grace over his food. When he looked up again, reaching for a crisp triangle of fried-corn tortilla, she was sitting with both shoulders pressed to the back of her seat, her mouth compressed in a straight line.

"What's wrong?"

"I…were you *praying* just then?"

"Yeah. What of it?"

"Nothing." She shook her head and glanced around. "So you're, like, a God freak or something?"

"You could say that. What about you? Aren't you a believer?"

His stomach muscles clenched as he waited for her answer.

"Yeah, I am." She did that thing with her bangs, and then she positively astounded him, muttering, "Actually, my brother's a minister."

"No kidding!"

She nodded, then looked away and back again.

"I never asked you, how do you like your shirts done?"

The abrupt change in subject startled him.

"Oh. Uh."

"Starch?"

"Well…"

"They stay cleaner longer, but it takes extra time," she told him matter-of-factly. "Spray starch gives it a nice finish, but a lot of men like the extra weight and feel of the real thing."

"Spray starch is fine," he said, realizing that she was trying to avoid talking about her brother. Or God. Vince wasn't sure what to think about that. Either way, it troubled him, but since she was obviously unwilling to get into it, he had no choice but to let it go.

His stomach growled again, and he loaded up one of the chips, inviting her to help herself. They'd emptied the basket by the time the main course arrived, and he'd told her his sisters' names and those of his nieces and nephews, except the one on the way, but she hadn't said another word about her own family or much of anything else.

"So how'd you get into the car-repair business?" she asked as he cut up his plate-sized steak.

"Went to school, went to work, saved up some cash, made an investment. I reinvested that and started looking for a property. It grew from there."

She stabbed a piece of lettuce with her fork.

"You make it sound easy."

He shook his head, chewing the tender steak, and swallowed.

"Lots of hard work and pinching pennies."

She waved a fork around and asked, "You do this sort of thing all the time?"

"What sort of thing?"

"Bartering with people who can't afford to pay cash for their car repairs."

He shrugged. "It seems a good way to take care of the problem."

"Seems chancy to me. How do you know you're coming out even?"

He laid down his knife and fork and rested his forearms on the table. "Listen, I'm not ashamed to say that I've worked hard because I have, but the truth is that I've been very richly blessed in life, too. It would be pretty selfish and self-centered of me not to try to work with folks who haven't had my breaks. Don't you think?"

"Yeah," she admitted bluntly, "I do."

He chuckled at her refreshing honesty and got down to some serious eating.

At least they agreed on *something*. So what if she was wary and kept her distance? Maybe she wasn't a "God freak," as she'd put it. She obviously had some standards, and that was okay by him.

If his stomach muscles sometimes clenched around her, well, he'd figure out what that meant later. Meanwhile, they were both getting their needs met. She needed her car in good running order; he needed his laundry done. And maybe they could help each other in additional ways, too. Time would tell.

"About Monday," he said, preparing to step out of her car in front of his office, "I'll be there to let you in, and if I'm not there when you need to leave, you can just lock up on your way out."

"All right."

"Meanwhile, I'll expect you to drop the car by on Saturday morning to get those hoses changed."

She nodded. "I'll do that." He had his head out the door when she impulsively stopped him. "By the way…" He relaxed back into his seat and turned to face her.

"Yeah?"

She felt awkward saying it, but she knew it was the right thing to do.

"I wanted to thank you. For everything. I—Including dinner. I really didn't expect you to buy."

He smiled. "No biggie. Consider it my way of apologizing for failing to tell you up front that you'd be working at my house."

"All right."

"That mean I'm forgiven?"

"Let's just say I'm willing to overlook your lapse in judgment. Again."

"Ouch."

She laughed, so he wouldn't figure it was too big a lapse in her estimation.

"Take care now," he said, getting out of the car. He flipped her a jaunty wave and walked toward a big white pickup truck with the shop's name and information painted on the sides. Thoroughly bemused, Jolie put the car in gear and headed home.

She had to say this for Vincent Cutler. He was one of a kind. First he'd frightened her, then he'd charmed her, then angered her and then charmed her again. That ought to be a recipe for distrust and disaster, but somehow she felt that he was basically harmless. In fact, he seemed like a real nice guy.

More puzzling still, he seemed actually to like her, and she hadn't really given him anything much to like. That made her wonder if he didn't have a hidden agenda, but if he did, she couldn't figure out what it was. He didn't seem to be the self-righteous, pie-in-the-sky type that she'd too often found religious people—including her brother Marcus—to be. Then again, he didn't appear to be out for whatever he could get, either. He just seemed to be…well, so far as she could tell, he was just a really nice man, which, in more ways than one, was surprising.

For one thing, Vincent Cutler was a handsome man, and he had the easygoing self-confidence that all handsome men seemed to possess. In addition, he was ambitious, but in a hardworking, down-to-earth way, not at all as if he figured the world owed him success for being what he was.

It didn't quite seem fair that on top of all that he should also be nice. Could be for show, of course. He might be the most clever of con men, but somehow she didn't think so.

She owed him money, and he was willing to barter for services rendered, but what assurance did he have that she'd even bother to show up for work? The majority of the repairs that her car needed were already done, and since she hadn't actually authorized any of them, she could pretty much tell him to take a leap if she was of a mind to, which she was not.

So, okay, she had to figure that he was a good judge of people, too, but that didn't explain why he'd done what he had. He'd fixed her car, knowing that she very probably would not be able to pay him and had not authorized the work but would likely try to do the right thing. That made him kind, willing to take a chance and a good judge of character.

His list of attributes was getting longer all the time, not that it mattered one tiny whit. She honestly didn't expect to see him much after tonight. They'd made their bargain, and she would fulfill her end as he'd already done his, and that would be that. Wouldn't it?

Somehow she sensed a flaw in her reasoning.

All right, so she'd be working in his house. That didn't mean he'd have the time or the inclination to babysit her. The man had a business to run, and obviously he wasn't worried about her stealing from him. Why should he? She was no thief.

Of course, he couldn't know that at this point. But she couldn't very well steal a house, and she hadn't seen much inside worth the taking, which made it all the more remarkable, even suspect, that he was willing to go out on a limb for somebody like her.

What did he hope to get out of it? Except a fair exchange of services, that is.

Truth to tell, she just didn't know what to make of Vince Cutler, and maybe she never would. What did it matter anyway, so long as her car was running well and she wasn't choosing between eating and paying a mechanic's bill?

It should not have mattered at all.

But somehow it did.

She told herself that she didn't like surprises, that the world was easier to navigate if people just stayed in their assigned boxes and did what was expected of them. The truth was, though, that Vincent Cutler was turning out to be something of a godsend, and she really didn't want to think about that.

After all, if God was looking out for her, how did she explain losing Russell?

Chapter Five

When he opened his door to her on Monday morning Vince couldn't help smiling. She just looked so good standing there in her simple jeans and a faded red tank top under a soft yellow, short-sleeved shirt hanging open down the front. Her biscuit-gold hair, loose except for the narrow band that held it neatly behind her ears, flowed down her back. Without so much as a dab of makeup or a single piece of jewelry, and dressed for a day of real work, she still managed to look every inch a woman, a woman who was not best pleased, if her frown was any indication.

He supposed it had to do with the dirty, dark-blue shadow on his chin and jaws. His mother and sisters certainly scowled if he went around unshaven, but sometimes a fellow just couldn't face a razor in the morning, and Monday was the one day of the week when he didn't have to, provided, of course, that he didn't have errands to run or a meeting of some sort.

Today was such a day, which meant that he'd seen no reason to shave. Now, rubbing his prickly jaw with one hand, he wished he'd lathered up anyway.

Putting on the best face that he could under the circumstances, he broadened his smile and bade her a cheery, "Good morning."

"Morning," she muttered, glancing down at his bare feet before sliding past him into the foyer. "Am I too early?"

He closed the door. "Not at all. I like an early start on the day myself."

"Hmm, well, I'll just head to work and let you finish getting ready to leave."

His smile wilted.

"Uh, I'm not going anywhere."

Her chin jerked up, eyes wide as saucers.

"Not going anywhere?"

She couldn't have looked more appalled. Vince shifted his feet.

"Monday's my day off, too. Didn't I make that clear before?"

She folded her arms.

"Obviously not."

He brought his hands to his hips, fighting down a surge of irritation, though whether he was more irritated with himself or her he didn't know. How many times and in how many ways could he mess up with this woman?

"I guess I assumed, since we're both in service industries, that you'd naturally figure…" He broke off, reaching deep for patience. Grasping it, he said, "If it'll make you more comfortable, I'll find somewhere to go."

"Why don't you just do that, then," she retorted, lifting her chin so high that he found himself practically staring down her nostrils.

"Fine," he snapped. "If that's what it takes to make you happy."

Grinding his back teeth together, he stomped off toward the back of the house, across the den and through the shallow alcove that opened onto the master bedroom.

Of all the testy, high-handed, downright unfriendly women in the world, he told himself, Jolie Wheeler purely took the cake.

Ripping a shirt from a hanger in the large walk-in closet, Vince yanked it on over his white T-shirt then went to the dresser to locate a pair of clean white socks. Plopping down on the side of the bed, he jerked on one of the socks. He was about to poke his toes into the other when he heard the front doorbell chime again. Rising, he managed to get the second sock on and take a step toward the door in the same movement.

He hadn't even made the den when one of his sisters—Olivia, he thought, or maybe Sharon, he couldn't always tell the voices of the older two apart—called out, "Hey, Vince! You decent?"

Wincing, he answered. "Yeah."

Great, that was all he needed, his nosy sisters barging in right in the middle of another misunderstanding with Jolie.

He hurried into the den, relieved to see that Jolie was absent. Maybe she hadn't heard the commotion.

Helen, the sister just younger than him, walked into the den. Olivia, the sister just older than him, was on her heels.

"Where are your boots?" Olivia asked, as if he was a two-year-old who'd forgotten where he'd escaped from his shoes.

"Waiting for my feet," he told her dryly. "Actually I was just getting ready to leave."

Maybe that would get them on their way.

Fat chance.

They looked at each other and said in unison, "Hope it's not important."

Obviously no one was going anywhere anytime soon.

Vince stifled a sigh. His sisters were often exasperating, but they were all so crazy about him that he couldn't be unhappy to see any of them. Opening his arms, he wrapped each of them in a one-armed hug and quickly bussed their cheeks, hoping to get them on their way none the wiser.

Heaven knew what they'd think if they were to clap eyes on Jolie.

"Okay, what's up? You two are out and about awful early."

"Earlier than you," Helen teased, rubbing the spot where his unshaven chin had grazed her.

"Like I've never seen either of you running around at mid-morning in fuzzy slippers with curlers in your hair."

Helen chortled and Olivia sniffed, tossing her dark curls.

"That's different," Olivia argued. "I've got three boys to corral."

"And who's corralling those hooligans today?" he asked, grinning at the thought of his nephews.

"Mom."

"But she's got Bets to help her," Helen added with a grin. Vince laughed.

Four-year-old Elizabeth Ann, known affectionately

by the family as Bets, effectively commanded the co-
terie of Cutler grandchildren, numbering six in all. An
only child, to the growing dismay of her parents, she'd
never had any trouble holding her own against her five
older cousins, four of whom were boys.

Now that Donna, Vince's youngest sister, was expecting, however, Bets was showing signs of insecurity
at losing her position as the baby of the family. As a result, she'd become a bossy little termagant whose or-
ders the older five obeyed slavishly in an unspoken
conspiracy to reassure her.

The whole thing was rather sweet to behold and
would resolve itself, everyone was certain, in time.

"So what's got you two over here hassling me at this
early hour of the morning?" Vince tried again.

Olivia slipped out of his embrace and moved to the
center of the sparsely furnished room, holding out her
arms.

"Do you even have to ask? My goodness, Vince, you
might as well still be living in that little cracker box of
an apartment."

"This house needs proper furnishings," soft-spoken,
light-haired Helen added, leaning into him.

"And since you show no signs whatsoever of finding a wife to take care of the matter for you," Olivia began sternly, "we'll just have to do it."

Vince felt a spurt of panic. The very last thing he
wanted was his sisters outfitting his house for him. Just
the possibility made him shudder.

"Now, look here, sis—"

"Don't you look-here-sis me. I've wiped your snotty
nose, not to mention your—"

"Olivia!"

Undaunted, she wagged a finger at him.

"You still haven't bought so much as a throw rug! If we leave it to you, you'll be sitting here alone ten years from now on this same old ratty couch eating your supper out of a can. Now, the alone part you'll have to fix yourself—with God's help, of course—but the other we're willing and able to take care of. So, you can either come shopping with us, or we'll do it without you, whichever you prefer."

He rolled his eyes, preferring a hard jab with a hot poker to either alternative, and caught sight of Jolie's head easing around the casement of the kitchen door. An audacious idea burst into his mind, one he'd been mulling around in some fashion since he'd gotten a look at what she'd done with his old apartment. He knew that the idea was born of desperation and would likely blow up in his face, but he let it out anyway.

"As a matter of fact, that won't be necessary," he said calmly. "It's already in hand."

He beckoned Jolie, weighting the gesture with a hopeful look that he prayed his sisters would miss. She frowned at him but edged into the room, her cheeks a becoming shade of pink.

"I, uh, didn't find any color-safe bleach in the sack of supplies you left in the laundry room."

"No? Could've sworn I picked some up. I'm sure it was on your list."

Actually, he was positive that it was on her list of needed supplies and that he'd bought a big plastic tub of the stuff on his way home Saturday evening. It appeared that her curiosity had gotten the better of her and that she was too embarrassed to admit that fact, which suited him just fine in the present circumstances.

He waved her further into the room, saying to his sisters, "Girls, I'd like you to meet Jolie Kay Wheeler. She's helping me out around here."

Two heads pivoted and tilted. Jolie might have been a bug under a microscope, the way they were studying her. Vince cleared his throat.

"Jolie, these are two of my sisters. Olivia." He nudged the elder, and she jumped as if he'd stuck her with a hat pin. "And Helen."

His sisters looked at him, then each other and finally at Jolie again. Both melted into smiles.

Helen leaned forward slightly and asked in her sweetest voice, "Would that be *Miss* Wheeler?"

"Uh. Um-hm."

Suddenly those smiles were beaming around the room with the force of a lighthouse on a dark and moonless night at sea, and the next thing Vince knew, they'd swarmed her like a pack of locusts, both chirping at once.

"Oh, it's so nice to meet you!"

"He hasn't said a word, the brat. We spoiled him rotten, you know, only boy and all that."

"But he's really very sweet, not half as stubborn as he seems. A little impulsive, maybe, but manageable."

Vince rolled his eyes at that, but no one paid him the least mind.

"Are you a professional decorator?" Helen asked.

"Have you known each other long?" Olivia wanted to know.

"All right, all right."

Vince waded into the fray and rescued Jolie with a hand firmly cupping her elbow to draw her to his side. She glared daggers up at him, and he could see the demand in her eyes. What was going on?

He tried to think of a way to explain it and came up only with the truth. "I, uh, I've been meaning to ask you if you'd help me outfit this place. I mean, yours looks so great." He shot a desperate volley at his sisters, saying, "I really love what she's done with her apartment. It's just my kind of thing, you know? Very tasteful, very…chic."

He wouldn't know chic if it bit him, but he didn't think it involved being upholstered in chintz or layered with doilies.

Jolie stared at him for a full five seconds before she slowly asked, "You want *me* to help you furnish and decorate this place?"

"Yeah. Sure. Absolutely."

She put a finger to her chest. *"Me?"*

"I know it's a lot to ask," he told her, instinctively pulling her closer, both elbows cupped in his hands now. "But I really like the look of your apartment. I like it better than anything else I've seen. And I *really* need the help." He slid a glance over her head toward his sisters before bringing it back to plumb those soft jade eyes. "Please."

Jolie dropped her gaze, lifted a shoulder in a casual shrug, and lightly conceded, "Okay."

He could have kissed her. He might have kissed her, if his sisters hadn't been standing there grinning like idiots and soaking up the whole thing. As it was, his right hand just sort of slipped around to the center of her back, finding its way beneath the heavy, silken fall of her hair.

He beamed at his sisters.

"See. Good as done."

They ignored him, as usual.

"Now, sugar," Olivia said to Jolie, stepping closer, "if you need anything at all, you just give a yell. All four of us would be delighted to pitch in and help out."

Jolie inched closer to Vince, apparently intimidated by the gleam in his sister's eyes. What could he do but slide his arm around her? He couldn't help noticing that she was a perfect fit.

"In fact," Helen was saying, "why don't you come to dinner on Sunday so we can talk about it all together? Mama would be thrilled, wouldn't she, Vince?"

"Oh, uh, sure."

It was the bald truth, never mind that what his sisters were assuming was not.

"I—I couldn't intrude," Jolie said, obviously unprepared for this full-frontal assault.

"No intrusion!" Olivia exclaimed, seizing and squeezing both of Jolie's hands. "Really, the whole family would be thrilled." She abruptly switched tactics. "Make her come, Vince."

"Oh, please come," Helen added to Jolie.

"All right. Okay. Enough," Vince interrupted firmly, literally putting himself between Jolie and his sisters. "I'll take it from here." He reached out and started sweeping them toward the door with one arm. "Thanks, girls. I appreciate your stopping by, but frankly you're holding up the show now, so if you don't mind…"

"Yeah, yeah, we're going," Olivia conceded drolly.

She pecked him on the cheek and strode for the entry, beckoning Helen to follow. Helen paused long enough to go up on tiptoe and throw her arms around Vince's neck. He bent forward to accept her kiss and hear her whisper in his ear.

"I'm so glad. She's very pretty."

"Umm," he answered noncommittally, feeling terrible about misleading them and ironically pleased at how it had gone so far.

"It was very nice to meet you, Jolie," Helen said with a last smile in Jolie's direction.

With her light-brown hair and dark-blue eyes, Helen was the sweetest and most soft-hearted of his sisters and at times his favorite, though he could say the latter of all of them at various moments.

"Nice to meet you, too," Jolie murmured, nodding.

It struck Vince that she actually meant it, and an unexpected feeling of warmth swirled through him. He sent her a grateful look and hurried after his sisters to see them safely out.

He knew that the whole family would soon be thinking, as Olivia and Helen must, that Jolie was his girlfriend, which meant they'd naturally assume that they would see her on Sunday at dinner, and he wouldn't disabuse them of that notion. Yet.

He didn't mean to lie to them. He'd just make the truth clear to them a little later, like after he'd gotten Jolie to agree to help him out. He really did want, need, her help decorating and furnishing his house, and who knew? She might even be willing to come over to his mom's for Sunday dinner. Wouldn't hurt to ask. He hoped.

Jolie stood right where he'd left her until he returned from seeing his sisters out. She'd gotten over her embarrassment at being caught eavesdropping—mostly, anyway. When she'd heard the doorbell and then female voices, curiosity had simply gotten the better of her.

For a moment she'd thought that some girlfriend, or

two, had come to call, but she'd quickly realized that they were his sisters. It had become obvious that he didn't want them decorating his house, and she hadn't minded helping him out with that, but of course, he wasn't serious about her doing it. Was he?

She couldn't imagine what had made him desperate enough even to suggest such a thing.

"So what's the deal with your sisters outfitting this place?" she demanded the moment that he reentered the room.

"None at all," he said quite happily, "that's the point."

She glanced at the battered, mismatched furnishings in the room.

"No offense, but you could use some help, not to mention some decent furniture."

"Don't I know it, but not from my family. And with you to help me, they won't have to."

"But you don't really want me to help you furnish and decorate this place," she said confidently, only to watch his face rearrange itself into a blank mask.

"That mean you're backing out on me?"

She gaped in astonishment. He really meant it!

"I'm not a professional decorator," she pointed out.

"So what? Neither are any of them."

"That's not the issue!"

"What is the issue?" he asked sharply. Then, before she could even answer, he turned out both palms beseechingly. "Look, I'll pay you for your help. All right? How would that be?"

"But I'm not a professional decorator!" she repeated, more forcefully this time in case he'd missed it the first.

"I know that!" he retorted. "I don't want a professional decorator. I want a helping hand from someone whose taste I appreciate."

What was he talking about? She didn't have any taste; she couldn't afford *taste*.

Didn't he understand that she'd never had two whole nickels to rub together? Whatever "decorating" she'd done at her place she'd managed with old sheets and stuff. It was all done of necessity. She'd never had the luxury of actually picking out things.

Her world was one of make-do. His was... She looked around her and gulped. This house was a palace, an empty palace.

"You can't mean it."

He thumped the side of his head with the heel of one hand and muttered at the far wall, "I know I'm speaking English, so it couldn't have gotten lost in translation."

She parked her hands at her hips, too astonished to take issue with his jibes.

"You actually *do* mean it."

"Hello! Houston, we have contact."

She flattened her lips and narrowed her eyes at him to let him know that he wasn't funny, at least not to her, but her heart was suddenly racing.

"I don't get it. You've got family ready, willing and able to help you. Why ask *me?*"

"Because I've got family ready, willing and insisting on helping me."

She noted that he had not said able.

He sighed gustily.

"Have you ever seen those old fifties movies where the walls are all papered in big bouquets of flowers and even the lampshades have ruffles on them?"

Jolie made a face, disliking the picture he'd created in her mind.

"I love my mom dearly," he went on, "but she has never met a doily or a chintz pattern that she didn't like. As for my sisters, it's the same song just different verses. They've all got their themes, you know? With Sharon, it's chickens."

"Chickens?" Jolie echoed, eyebrows rising.

"Chickens everywhere," he told her. "The throw pillows in the living room have chickens on them. Chicken-patterned chintz."

He shuddered, and Jolie's mouth twitched.

"With Olivia, it's cows," he went on blandly, "black-and-white cows. Black-and-white cows with red in the kitchen, black-and-white cows with blue in the living room, black-and-white cows with green in the bedroom. Black-and-white cows with yellow in the bath. My brother-in-law swears that late at night he can hear mooing."

Jolie snickered and clapped a hand over her mouth, but despite his woebegone expression, he seemed to be enjoying himself.

"Helen, now, Helen's more sedate," he said. "Helen's whole house is tan. Even the flowers on her chintz sofa are tan. The flowers on the wallpaper are tan. The flowers on the throw rugs are tan."

"Oh, no." Jolie bit down on a sputter of laughter.

"But Donna," he managed to say, despite his own grin, "she's the avant-garde one. Her chintz is polka-dotted. Navy blue on white. Or white on navy blue for contrast."

Jolie guffawed, imagining his house done up in flowered chickens and polka-dotted cows in every color of the rainbow. With doilies.

"S-so you can s-see my problem," he chortled. Swallowing, he managed a serious tone. "Hey, I'm just trying to avoid hurt feelings. And chintz of any sort."

He shuddered spastically, and Jolie nearly fell over, laughing so hard that her sides hurt. He threw an arm around her for support, burbling and bumping hips with her.

"I—I'm a desperate man," he managed, sucking air.

After a moment they both calmed somewhat.

He caught a breath and wiped an eye, saying, "I really don't want to have to hire a professional. I don't want a showplace. I want something homey and comfortable but *me,* and I know I'm more apt to get that with you than with any of them. For one thing, I can be honest with you."

She nodded and dabbed at her eyes with the back of one wrist.

"Okay, I get it now."

He clapped his hands together and turned his face up to the ceiling.

"Thank You, God."

She shoved an elbow into his ribs.

"Get serious."

"Sweetheart, I *am* serious," he told her, sounding it.

She ignored the *sweetheart* part—just a figure of speech, after all—and the little thrill that came with it, concentrating instead on studying her surroundings. She discovered, to her surprise, that she really wanted to do this thing.

Suddenly, her mind was hopping with ideas.

"I just don't know how much good I can do for you," she admitted forthrightly. "I don't have much experience."

"You've got style, though, and it more or less mirrors mine, or what I'd like mine to be, anyway. And I meant what I said about paying you."

She shook her head. "I can't take money for something I'm not trained or qualified to do."

He held out both hands again, this time in a stalling motion. Then he snapped his fingers.

"Tell you what, let's stick with the barter plan. I'll give you a year, make that two years, of free automobile upkeep for your help."

Her eyes widened, but before she could reply to that generous offer, he held up an index finger.

"This time, though, there are strings attached."

She grinned.

"Let me guess. No chintz."

"That's one, but there is another.

She folded her arms in mock resignation.

"Let's hear it."

He dipped at the knees, scrunching up his face in a wheedling gesture.

"You have to come to dinner on Sunday."

Was that all? She opened her mouth to ask, but he hurried on.

"My family will be disappointed if you don't. The girls are used to getting their way, frankly, but they always mean well, and after refusing their help with the house, I just don't want to have to explain why I couldn't convince you to accept their invitation to Sunday dinner."

She was ready to capitulate after the first sentence, but she didn't let him know that. Vince Cutler groveling was a very pleasant experience.

"Well," she mused, stroking her chin, "I guess I could."

"Great!" He clapped his hands together. "How's this? I'll pick you up for church and afterward we'll go straight to Mom's."

Jolie frowned, suspicion instantly rearing its ugly head again.

"Church? Who said anything about church? I thought we were talking about dinner."

"Dinner's always first thing after church," he told her, matter-of-factly. "Mom usually puts something in the oven or slow-cooker before she leaves the house for services, and it's ready when she gets back."

Jolie bit her lip. What was it with this guy? Every time she thought she had him figured out, he threw her some sort of curve. Was this about his sisters' expectations, his empty house or getting her to church?

What was it with church people, anyway? They came on as caring, then turned on you. Marcus had.

"I don't know," she muttered, more to herself than to him.

"Fine," he said lightly. "I'll pick you up immediately after the service. Just be ready and waiting. Mom hates it when we're late to the table. It's her all-time pet peeve. But it's not too far from your place. If we hurry we'll be there in time."

Jolie figured she'd be nuts to refuse. Two years of no worries about her old car! Plus, she'd have the pleasure of outfitting this grand house.

She nodded decisively.

"Just tell me what time."

"Twelve o'clock noon," he told her, sounding relieved. He smacked his hands together again, rubbing them as he glanced around. "Oh, man, I can't wait to get started. When can we, do you think?"

She shrugged, considering.

"Well, I suppose we could do some preliminary window-shopping as soon as I get the laundry done."

"In that case," he exclaimed, turning toward the kitchen, "I'll help you."

"That's not necessary," she told him, laughing and hurrying to catch up as he strode off on stocking feet.

"I can at least help you sort," he insisted, forging ahead.

Jolie paused to roll her eyes. What kind of guy got this excited about decorating his house? In some ways, she was afraid to find out.

She swept into the laundry room to discover him knee-deep in the pile. He'd started tossing clothes every which way. She stood shaking her head, her hands on her hips, until he plopped a pale-blue dress shirt that would look stunning with his eyes into a pile of jeans. She plucked it out again, then started making a few more corrections, and somehow they fell into a pattern.

Before she knew it, they were standing side by side at the work table treating stains at her direction with one of a trio of products.

When the first load was ready, Vince picked it up and stuffed it into the washer while she measured the correct amount of liquid detergent. She poured it into the dispenser and turned some knobs to adjust the water temperature; then he pushed a button, and water started to fill the tub.

An odd sense of satisfaction settled over her, but she didn't have long to enjoy it. He grabbed her hand and tugged her toward the door.

"Come on," he said, "I want to show you the rest of the house."

She put on a smile, nodded and prepared to be delighted, but that had nothing whatsoever to do with Vince. It was strictly about his house and the unexpected pleasure of getting her hands on it. At least that's what she told herself.

Chapter Six

"Might as well start at the beginning," Vince said, dropping her hand.

He felt all too aware of her for some reason, but he simply wouldn't think about it: better to concentrate on the house.

"You've probably guessed that this big empty space at the front is supposed to be formal living and dining," he quipped, then went on to explain, "I wanted everything open for entertaining, you know? This way, even the entry, which is often just wasted space, becomes a part of the whole, flowing right into the den with the beverage bar and, of course, the kitchen. At Mom and Dad's we're always hanging out in the kitchen."

He glanced over his shoulder as they passed beneath one of a pair of tall, wide arches that opened off the foyer. Leading her to the center of the long space, he let her take the room's measure.

"You could hold a ball in here!" she finally exclaimed.

"I don't think it's that big," he muttered sheepishly.

Smiling, he pointed out what seemed to him to be the salient architectural touches.

"The set-backs are perfect for displaying things, figurines maybe or…I don't know."

"Plants," she mused, looking over the nooks and crannies that stair-stepped up the front wall, creating a deep inset for the tall, multipaned window, "and maybe some pottery."

"I like the look of leaded glass," he went on, drawing her attention to the window itself, "but I didn't want anything too formal, so we went with this oxidized surface on the metal parts." He chuckled. "Mom says rust is not a decorative finish, but I think it looks cool."

"Like it's been around a long time and will be forever," Jolie commented, lightly brushing her fingertips over the window casing.

He couldn't have been more pleased.

"That's it. That's it exactly. Besides it just seems more…" He curved his hands, trying to grasp the right word.

"Masculine," Jolie supplied.

He felt a tiny shock at that. He hadn't realized that was the effect that he'd been going for until now.

"Yeah. Yeah, it is at that."

"Which means we can throw in a little elegance without making the room too feminine."

He liked that thought. Elegant but not frilly.

"That sounds right. Now, back here…"

He hurried her across the foyer and into the hall branching off it.

"This first door, that's the powder room."

She craned her neck around a bit before he herded her away.

"These three rooms on the front are bedrooms. The first two share a bath."

Walking her through quickly, he threw open empty closets and pointed out the window seats before moving back into the hall.

"The last one here at the end I think of as the guest room because it has its own bath."

He let her look around for a moment, though the room was basically an empty box with a nice window. The small bath contained a tub with a shower in it, unlike the other two full baths in the house, which boasted both tubs and shower stalls.

They started back down the hall on the other side, toward the powder room.

"This," he said, pushing wide double doors, "is what I call the study."

It was a long room with a single window in the end, lots of bare bookcases and two built-in desks. A computer sat rather forlornly atop one, but he hadn't gotten around to hooking it up yet. Didn't see the point until he at least got a desk chair. Jolie wandered into the room, her jaw dropping.

"You have your own library!"

"I would if I had any books," he said. "I thought this would be a good place for the kids to do their homework and maybe play some video games, that sort of thing."

"Kids!" she exclaimed, whirling on him. "You have *kids?*"

For a moment he wasn't sure what she was asking. Maybe she wondered if he *wanted* kids. Or was she saying that she didn't want them? Then again, it was a pretty straightforward question, even if it didn't make any sense.

"Of course not. How can I have kids when I'm not even married?"

She literally snorted.

"In case you haven't noticed, you don't have to be married to have children."

"*I* do," he stated flatly, frowning.

She stared at him for several seconds, as if verifying the truth of what he'd just said.

Apparently satisfied, she nodded briskly and swept past him, muttering, "Good for you."

His jaw descended. Had he seen the sheen of tears in her eyes? Before he could think better of it, he went after her, catching her by the elbow just as she reached the foyer.

"Jolie, are you okay?"

She nodded, but she didn't look at him.

"I guess it's your religion that makes you think like that. Lots of men don't."

"It's my faith, yes," he said, "but it's common sense, too. Plenty of men feel the same way. They know that children should have two parents."

"But lots of them don't."

"And most of them turn out fine," he conceded, "but it means twice the effort for a single parent."

"True." It came out barely more than a whisper.

He caught her chin with the crook of his fingers and angled her face so he could gauge her expression. For a moment she stood with her eyes downcast before suddenly lifting her eyelids. The jade of her irises sparkled with tears.

"Jolie?"

He was almost afraid to ask why she cried, but she pulled away from him and gave him an answer anyway.

"My sister has a little boy." Her voice cracked at the end. "His father's in prison for killing an off-duty policeman during a robbery."

Vince pushed a hand over his face, horribly relieved even as he drawled, "Aw, Jolie, I'm sorry to hear that."

"Russell's better off never knowing him," she asserted defiantly.

"I'm even more sorry about that," Vince said quietly.

She turned away then, and he watched that steel rod slide into her spine.

"We don't all get the ideal parents," she told him almost grudgingly.

He wondered about her parents, but he didn't think asking would get him anywhere just then, not with her defenses back in place.

"I'm sure there are times," he said carefully, "when one parent is better than two. I was speaking in generalizations before."

"I know." She glanced at him and moved away, mumbling, "I should check the laundry."

"Sure. We can finish the tour later. There's just the master suite."

He stood there until she disappeared into the kitchen, then he sighed and jammed his hands into his pockets.

What would he have done, what would he have said, if it had been her and not her sister? It wasn't his place to judge, of course, but he did believe that his values were right, and it made his belly burn to think that she might have been used by some man and then abandoned by him.

He went into the living room and sat down to think, but Jolie Wheeler couldn't be puzzled out with what little information he had. He bowed his head and let the Spirit guide his prayer.

He asked God why Jolie Wheeler was suddenly a part of his life. She'd said that her brother was a preacher, but she spoke about faith and God as if she didn't quite understand them, almost as if she carried certain resentments. Was he supposed to help her deal with that somehow? Or did God have something else entirely in mind?

There had been moments when he was showing her through the house just now, when being with her had felt exactly right. Then there were those moments of confusion, like now.

He shook his head, asking God not to let him do anything foolish until he had this thing figured out. Oh, and he could use some help keeping his temper, too, because she had a way of setting him on edge, which just went to show how confused he really was.

Vince rarely lost his temper, rarely even felt the emotion of anger, but he seemed prone to step wrong where she was concerned, and then the yelling started. He hadn't raised his voice to a woman other than his sisters in his whole life, and he hadn't done it with one of them since he was maybe fourteen.

What was it about Jolie Wheeler that got under his skin?

Jolie slipped into the kitchen some time later, not quite sure what she expected. It wasn't to find him making lunch.

"What are you doing?"

He turned a glance over one shoulder, smiled and waved a knife smeared with mustard.

"What does it look like I'm doing?"

She folded her arms, relieved at his bantering tone.

"It looks like you're building a wall with bread and meat."

"There's lettuce and tomato in there, too," he told her with mock defensiveness, nodding at the gargantuan sandwich, "and pickles and cheese and bell peppers, even some sliced mushrooms." He slid one half of the monstrosity to the side. "Hope you like mustard."

She blinked, oddly touched, and barely bit back the words, *For me?* They sounded mewling and pathetic even inside her head.

"You want to get that cantaloupe out of the fridge and carve it up?" he directed, pointing with his chin. "I'm in a cantaloupe mood. How about you?"

She walked over to the refrigerator and opened the door.

"I like cantaloupe."

"You can use that paring knife there on the counter," he said. "I rinsed it after I sliced the peppers. Oh, and grab that pitcher of iced tea. There's a bowl of sliced lemon in there, too. Got a white lid on it."

"I see it."

She placed everything on the counter, then carried the melon to the sink, where she split, cleaned, peeled and sliced it, dropping the crescent-moon-shaped slivers into a plastic bowl which Vince had set out for her. While she worked, he got down mismatched plastic tumblers and filled them with ice, tea and lemon, then put the sandwiches on plates and carried everything to the island in the center of the room.

Producing a bag of chips, he leaned a hip against the counter, munching, until she rinsed and dried her hands.

With a swipe of one foot, he pulled out a short, rather wobbly stool for her. Then he hopped up onto the counter and lifted his plate onto his lap.

"I could eat a horse," he said, spearing a piece of melon with a fork.

"Is that in here, too?" she teased, eyeing the sandwich mountain on her plate.

He didn't answer, and when she looked up, it was to find his head bowed. She quickly looked down again.

"We thank You, Lord," he said easily, "for Your many blessings. I especially thank You for saving me from the chintz squad and, most importantly, giving me a way to keep from hurting their feelings. You know I love them, Lord, and I know they mean well, so thank You for bringing Jolie along to help me out. Amen."

She didn't know what to think about him mentioning her in his prayer, but what she said was, "Do you always do that?"

"Pray before I eat?" he asked, and quickly devoured the melon slice in two bites. "Yep. Don't you?"

She answered him honestly, but for some reason it made her uncomfortable.

"No."

"How come?" He wrapped his hands around the enormous sandwich. "Wasn't it the done thing at your house?"

"I never had a house," she blurted.

He lowered the sandwich.

"Around your home then."

"Can't say as I really ever had one of those, either."

"You had to grow up somewhere."

She picked up her own sandwich and took a bite just so she couldn't answer him. He did not, however, let the subject drop, just changed his tack.

"Guess your folks weren't the praying kind."

"Wouldn't know. Probably not."

"How is it you don't know something like that?" he asked softly, shifting his plate to the countertop.

She felt her shoulders lift in a shrug, and that was when she knew she was going to answer.

"Never even met my father," she said with a swallow, "and Mom was gone at least half the time."

"Where was she gone to?"

She studied her sandwich, but in truth, her appetite had disappeared.

"The better question is *who* was she gone *with*."

"Who?"

His voice could be so gentle, so warm, sometimes. It made her own sound harsh and sharp.

"Some man or other."

He said nothing for a moment. Then he moved his plate to his lap again and picked up his sandwich.

"Who raised you then?"

She picked a pickle slice out of the sandwich and popped it into her mouth.

"The system."

"The system?" he echoed.

"The state. Child Welfare."

"Ah. I have a real good buddy who was raised in foster homes. You met him, I think. Boyd."

She looked up in surprise, and he bit off a huge chunk of sandwich.

"Wasn't he the guy who towed my car?"

Vince nodded.

"Doesn't he work for you?"

"Um-hm."

"And you still call him a real good buddy?"

He worked the food in his mouth and swallowed.

"What's so odd about that? We were friends before he came to work for me."

They were both aware that she was steering the conversation away from her and back to him, but Vince didn't seem to mind. She let herself relax somewhat.

"Isn't it hard to keep the business part separated from the friendship part?"

"Don't know," he said succinctly, readying his sandwich for another assault. "Never tried."

She rolled her eyes, suddenly enjoying herself again.

"Now that's some attitude for a business owner."

"What's wrong with it?"

"What's wrong with it? Somebody has to be the boss, that's what's wrong with it."

"You sound just like Boyd. Sissy and I are always telling him that he's more concerned about my business than I am." He chuckled.

"Who's Sissy?"

"Boyd's wife. We grew up together, Sissy and me. She ran tame with my sisters, Helen and Donna. You probably wouldn't like her. She's sweet as sugar and soft-spoken as a running brook."

Jolie huffed, knowing full well that she was being baited but enjoying herself too much to care.

"I have been insulted. You have just insulted me, Vince Cutler."

He laughed and leaned forward, confessing, "Actually, she spits and hisses just about as much as you. The two of you would either get on like a house afire or you'd rip each other to shreds, and I'm not taking bets on which." He winked then and added, "But she's not as cute as you are."

With that he hopped down from the counter and carried his plate across the room, where he ripped a paper towel from the roll and proceeded to wrap his sandwich for easier handling.

Jolie inwardly sputtered for a moment, but then she blinked and let an unfamiliar feeling wash over her.

Cute. He'd as much as said she was cute.

She began pulling the filling from between the slices of bread, poking it into her mouth bit by bit, and found that it was difficult to chew and smile at the same time.

"I've been thinking about it," Vince said, checking his rearview mirror, "and we don't really have to do those two bedrooms up front. Let's concentrate on the living and dining room for now, and then the den and kitchen."

"That's fine," Jolie said, feeling as though she was sitting on top of the world there in the cab of that big, brutish pickup truck.

She didn't like leaving the laundry unfinished to go shopping, but Vince Cutler could be *very* persuasive. She didn't even like to think how persuasive he could be, so she put her mind on the business at hand.

"However," she said, "the first thing you should do is get some drapes up, especially in those two front bedrooms. Until you get those windows covered, the house is going to look empty from the street."

"I hadn't considered that." He rubbed his cleanly shaven chin, glancing at her. "Where do we find them?"

Jolie considered a moment.

"I've heard there's a store down on Camp Bowie that specializes in window treatments."

"Camp Bowie it is."

"I don't suppose you know the measurements of the windows?" she asked hopefully.

He shook his head. "Not off hand, no, but I think I'm still carrying around a set of house plans tucked behind the back seat."

"Then I'd say we're in business," she told him confidently.

Famous last words.

It turned out that the windows in Vincent's custom-built house were not standard sizes. A persistent questioning of store personnel elicited the name of a custom draper, who was only too happy to show them styles and fabrics and quote prices, astonishingly high prices to Jolie's mind. In just over two hours at the draper's shop, however, they gained a good idea of what it was going to take to get the windows covered, but they were no closer to actually having done so.

"I think I'm going to have to put together a budget," Vince said thoughtfully, letting the shop door close behind him.

"A budget's good," Jolie agreed, moving across the sidewalk to the truck, which was parked directly in front of the building. The prices of custom-made draperies had shocked her, and her mind was reeling in search of alternatives. "You know, I've got an old sewing machine that I picked up at a garage sale. It's not fancy, but it does a good job, and I've been sewing up curtains and such for years now. Maybe I should—"

Vince cut her off in midthought. "Nope."

He stepped up to her side, and she frowned at him. "No? Why not? You saw the price of those things."

"Yes, I did, and they're high, but there are other drapery shops." He lifted one booted foot to the front bumper of the truck and balanced his forearms atop his knee. "Besides—and I don't mean any offense—I want this done right *and* quick. Now, I know you'd do good work, but you don't have time for sewing. You're already working three jobs, remember?"

Four counting the extra ironing, she thought, and one of them she'd left unfinished. Piles of laundry waited for the washer back at his house. Still…

"It's going to cost an awful lot of money."

"I'm aware of that. I figure at this point maybe five thousand for window treatments and three, maybe four, times that much for furnishings."

Several seconds passed before Jolie realized her mouth was hanging open. Even then some effort was required to snap it shut again, and she had to swallow before she could speak.

"That's your idea of a budget?"

He dropped his foot to the ground.

"I told you, I want it done right. I'm looking for quality, classic furnishings that won't need upgrading every couple years."

"And you're just going to toss me that much money and expect me to produce what you're looking for?"

"No," he said reasonably, "I intend to oversee every purchase. I want you to tell me what works best where."

She let out a long, slow breath.

"Man, oh, man. Did you ever pick the wrong girl for this job. That's more money than I've made in the past year."

"Jolie," he told her, "I've been planning and saving a long time for this, and I want to get it right. Your job is to tell me what you think will look good. I know what

I like, but I'm not sure which of the things I like will go together."

She shook her head, insisting, "You ought to hire a professional."

"We've been through this. I don't want a professional." He strode for the driver's door, fishing in his jeans pocket for his keys. "Now are you getting in or are we camping on the sidewalk?"

She got in.

"Want to take a look at some furniture?"

"Guess it won't hurt to look," she muttered.

Wrong again.

They hit four different stores before a helpful salesman finally directed them to a place that actually carried the rustic Western style that they both seemed to be envisioning. Vince declared the store perfect for their purposes the instant that they walked into the showroom, but Jolie took one look at the price of a leather sectional and insisted that they could do better elsewhere.

"I've seen handmade, one-of-a-kind pieces in this very style at the outdoor market for half the price," she hissed.

"What outdoor market?" he asked in hushed tones.

"Over in Dallas, downtown in the warehouse district. They open these big sheds on the weekends, and the artisans and craftsmen haul in their goods." Vince looked down at his toes. "I can get a Friday off if I ask in advance," she whispered, all but pleading. "We can at least look."

He tucked his fingertips into his waistband, rocking back on his heels.

"This Friday?"

"I'll see," she promised. "Maybe. I haven't had to ask off lately." She held back a wince at that. She hadn't had to take time off from work since she'd lost Russ. Pushing aside thoughts of her nephew, she fixed her mind on the issue at hand. "I'm sure I can get at least half a day."

Vince caught her arm and steered her toward the door, calling out to the anxious salesman, "Gotta run. We'll catch you later. Thanks for your help."

"I don't know why I didn't think of it sooner," she said once they reached the sidewalk. "I guess I didn't know exactly what you were looking for until you honed in on that last piece."

"Now that," he said, hooking a thumb over his shoulder, "is my idea of a comfy couch. It seats six and has recliners in each end."

"Two pieces would be easier to shift around," she pointed out cautiously. "Besides, that's better suited to the den than a so-called formal living room."

"Hmm, maybe you're right about that. See there." He beamed at her. "You do know what you're doing."

She turned away, rolling her eyes.

"Can I get back to some real work now?"

He chuckled, following her across the parking lot.

"You act like that laundry is going somewhere."

"Not unless I get it done, it isn't."

He unlocked the door and handed her up into the tall cab before making his way around to the driver's seat.

"You'd think we were spending *your* hard-earned cash," he teased.

"Yours is not as hard-earned as mine is or you'd feel the same way," she grumbled.

He shook his head and drove her back to his house,

where he busied himself elsewhere while she worked at the laundry and envisioned, room by room, what she really wanted to do with the place. It didn't take long for her to realize that what she needed was a comprehensive list of what it would take to achieve the look she was after. Just knowing how much money she had to play with set her imagination whirling.

She hadn't realized what fun simple dreaming could be.

Chapter Seven

Jolie was at the ironing board, down to the last dozen shirts in need of pressing, with a load of laundry in the washer, another in the dryer and two more still heaped on the floor, when Vince strolled into the room.

"Enough," he ordered. "The rest can wait."

She straightened to work a kink out of her back.

"At the very least, the pants have to be hung or they'll wrinkle and need pressing, too. And the towels have to go into the dryer before I can leave."

"Okay, I'll help you finish up. Then I want you to get out of here," he ordered, "or else I'm going to make you dinner."

"Ooh," she quipped, shuddering theatrically, "how diabolical."

"I should inform you that the sandwich constitutes the sum of my kitchen skills."

"Yuh," she said, perfectly serious, "how diabolical."

"It wasn't that bad!"

She giggled. "It wasn't bad at all, especially if you

happen to be a giant—or eat like one. But I couldn't let you feed me twice in one day."

"I don't see why not."

"Meals are not part of our deal, that's why not."

"Speaking of that," he began, "I think we ought to approach this new project from a different angle. What do you think about making a list of everything we know we're going to need and—" He broke off when she burst out laughing.

"That's just what I've been doing." She tapped her temple with the tip of one forefinger. "Just haven't got it down on paper yet."

"There you go," he said, grinning. "Great minds thinking alike."

"I don't know about that," she retorted playfully, "but I have a suggestion. Why don't you make your list, and I'll make mine, and on Friday we'll compare them, provided I can get time off from the cleaners."

"Sounds good to me. Then on Sunday we'll have something to show the girls. You do remember that Sunday comes with a meal, don't you?"

"Of course I remember."

"I see, so it's okay for my mom to feed you but not me. I think that's some sort of double standard."

She rolled her eyes. "It's not about the meal. It's about showing your family that you're making headway on furnishing this house."

"Don't be surprised if you have to make a progress report."

"That I'll leave to you."

The buzzer on the dryer went off, indicating that the load was finished, and she hurried to pull out the uniform pants before they could wrinkle.

He went for the rolling rack of hangers, saying, "So I'll pick you up at the cleaners about noon on Friday unless you call to cancel. Right?"

"Right. I'll have my list on paper by then."

"Me, too."

They worked for several minutes, folding, creasing and hanging the pants. The washer stopped before they were finished, and Jolie shifted that load into the dryer. All in all, it had been some day.

"Take off now," he ordered, "and I'll see you Friday."

"Yes, sir, boss, sir."

He brought his hands to his hips in a sarcastic pose.

"Right. You and Boyd, great respecters of my authority."

She just grinned, unplugged the iron and gathered up her handbag and keys.

"See ya." She turned for the door.

"Hey, Jolie."

She whirled in midstride.

"Yeah?"

He rocked back on his heels, gaze targeted on his toes. Then he looked up at her from beneath the smooth jut of his brow.

"Just wanted to say that I'm glad you moved into my old apartment. And got overloaded with my mail. And needed work on your car and…you know, all the rest."

Warmth spiraled through her, followed quickly by a spike of pure fear. She was getting caught up in something that she didn't quite understand here, and she wasn't sure how to feel about it, so she just nodded and went on her way.

It would have been a lot easier to deal with if she

could have convinced herself that she wasn't glad about how things had turned out, too.

They spent an hour at a table in a favorite chain restaurant of his, comparing their lists and debating the contents until they came up with a master list. The girl was nothing if not stubborn—and close with a buck.

Since it was his buck that she was wringing, Vince couldn't be too put out about her thrifty ways, especially since it was a habit which she obviously had developed from pure necessity. Strangely enough, that only made him want to spend more, either to irritate her or to delight her, he wasn't entirely sure which.

The tentative excitement lighting her eyes when she talked about actually picking out articles for purchase seemed reason enough to splurge all by itself, but he couldn't deny that arguing with her had become something of a favorite pastime, especially once he'd figured out that her tough exterior was just that, a front that she used to protect herself.

The question became by what, or whom, did she feel threatened?

Vince had no answers for that, but he exercised his better judgment and curbed the impulse to dump wads of cash on her, sensing that she wouldn't find the actual spending of it as enjoyable as he would find watching her spend it. That didn't mean that he wasn't tickled by her building enthusiasm for the project, however, and try as she might, she couldn't hide the evidence of it. At times, she practically bubbled, and it was in those moments that Vince found himself almost aching for the woman he glimpsed behind those jade eyes.

They spent the balance of the afternoon in Dallas

wandering around old warehouses and new sheet metal barns. The mid-November weather was glorious, with bright sunshine overhead and air crisp enough to feel like autumn while requiring nothing more onerous than a sweater or light jacket. It was Vincent's favorite time of the year in Texas.

The suffocating heat of summer had waned with September and the weather had run mild for weeks, gradually cooling. The trees were ablaze still, though some of the leaves had started to fall, but the weather would hold, maybe even right up into December, when the temperatures would take a plunge. Winter would bring one or two ice storms, but they would be brief and would lack the danger of the spring tornado season.

Yes, autumn was the heavenly season in Texas, at least as far as Vince was concerned. Jolie called it "perfect shopping weather."

He liked what he saw at the market. Much of it was imported from Mexico and, to a lesser extent, other countries, but most of it came straight out of workshops in Texas or one of the surrounding states. He absolutely went nuts over an easy chair covered in deerhide, manufactured by a retired aerospace engineer in Fort Davis, west of the Pecos River. The vendor stuck a "Hold" sign on it for them, and they tore through the rest of the market putting together a complete roomful of furnishings built around that one chair.

Problem was, he wanted that chair in the den where he could relax in the evening and watch a little TV or read. Jolie carped about deviating from their plan, but he could be stubborn, too, and in the end he got his way without too much tussle. Then she found the perfect dining-room suite, which sent them off on another search for coordinating pieces.

Vince wasn't completely sold on the living-room stuff that she picked out, but the vendor assured them that anything they didn't love once it was installed in the house could be returned. They arranged for delivery on Monday, and before he knew what had hit him, Vince found himself the proud owner of half a houseful of brand-new, handcrafted furniture, for much less than he'd have paid in a regular retail store.

All in all, it had been a very productive day.

"Wait until the girls hear how much we've gotten accomplished," he said as he drove Jolie back toward her car at the cleaners.

Jolie chewed her lip for a moment before saying, "I hope they won't think I've been extravagant."

"If they think anybody's been extravagant, it'll be me," he pointed out. "It's my house and my money, after all."

"Yes, but it's my plan."

"What difference does that make? I have final say. Besides it isn't any of their business."

"If you really believed that you wouldn't have insisted that I go to dinner on Sunday with your family."

"I didn't insist! I asked politely, and you kindly agreed." He narrowed his eyes at her. "You're not backing out on me, are you? Because I've already told Mom that you'll be there."

"Who said anything about backing out?" she demanded indignantly.

Vince laughed. He couldn't help it. Even their arguments—and they were constant but completely without rancor—engaged him in a way that no interaction with any other woman ever had. He fought the impulse to reach across the cab of the pickup and chuck her under the chin, but he couldn't deny himself the occasional glance.

She was growing on him, this Jolie Kay Wheeler, prickles and all. He found himself wondering if she might be the one, but then he reminded himself that he still knew little about her. God had not yet revealed His plan. Still, Vince couldn't deny a growing undercurrent of awareness between them. At least he suspected that it was mutual.

Then again, it wasn't wise to take anything for granted where Jolie was concerned.

Vince dropped Jolie off at her car behind the cleaners. It was later than they'd anticipated returning, so the rush hour was well past. He offered dinner, but Jolie said she had much to do. He didn't question her, but he did insist on following her home just to make certain that she got there safely.

She told him that he was a sexist, high-handed Neanderthal, and that she'd been taking care of herself for a quarter of a century at least, which prompted him to drawl, "I didn't think you were that old."

"I'm twenty-seven, thank you very much, and don't change the subject."

"And what is the subject? Oh, yeah, my gentlemanly impulse to see you safely to your own front door."

"Whatever," she replied with a huff, slamming the door to the cab.

He grinned, enjoying himself, and followed at a discreet distance until she turned her little jalopy into the apartment parking lot.

Twenty-seven, he mused. That seemed to him just

about the right age for a woman. Funny, but in some ways she seemed younger. And in some ways she seemed older. It was as if she maintained some measure of innocence while carrying the weight of the world on her slender shoulders.

"Lord," he prayed, "show me how to lighten her load."

She was trembling. He felt it in the hand that he placed at the small of her back as he began the first of many introductions to be made.

"Mom, Dad, this is Jolie Wheeler. Jolie, these are my parents, Ovida and Larry."

Jolie timidly offered her hand to his mother, who clasped it and held on for dear life as if afraid that her one chance for a daughter-in-law would escape before they could get her well and truly tied down.

"Sugar, you are as welcome as rain in the summer! My, isn't she a pretty thing, but of course Vince could always have his pick."

Vince groaned inwardly when Jolie shot him a startled glance. Why hadn't he set them all straight? He'd meant to, but somehow it hadn't seemed important. He should have realized that his mother would make her assumptions obvious. His dad had always said that Ovida was about as subtle as her flaming-red hair.

The hair that curled softly around her squarish face had faded over the years, but Ovida remained as bluntly spoken as ever. Vince cleared his throat, hoping she'd get the hint, and all but wrenched Jolie from her grasp, moving on to his eldest sister and her husband.

"This is Sharon and Wally and their two kids, Jack and Brenda. You've met Olivia, and this is her husband

Drew and their three boys, Mark, Matthew and Michael. Helen you also know. That wild man she's married to is John."

"Don't you believe a word of it," John put in, winking at Jolie and giving one corner of his beloved mustache a tweak.

Vince playfully tugged the other corner of his old running buddy's facial hair and kept going.

"The little redhead is Bets, and finally here's my baby sister Donna and her crackbrained other half Martin, whom we lovingly refer to as Chrome Dome."

Unperturbed at the teasing insult, Marty rubbed his perfectly bald head, wrapped his arms around his wife and patted her distended tummy, saying, "And this is either Anthony or Ann."

"We wanted to know which, but the baby didn't cooperate," Donna divulged, having inherited both her mother's red hair and frank manner. "Must take after Marty."

"Man, let's hope not," Vince retorted, straight-faced.

"Now, y'all get to the table," Ovida ordered. "The gravy's jelling."

The family turned en masse and swiftly moved into the dining room, leaving Vince and Jolie to bring up the rear. He dropped a reassuring smile on her, figured that he knew what her beetled brow was about and felt a hole open in the pit of his belly.

What on earth, he suddenly wondered, had possessed him to throw her into the arena with his family like this? He knew perfectly well that they all thought she was his girlfriend. It wasn't like him to exacerbate unfounded assumptions. Trouble was, he'd started thinking that maybe it shouldn't be unfounded.

The family scrambled for seats, leaving two places at the top of the *T* for him and Jolie. Vince had hoped that his mother would put the kids in the kitchen as usual, but instead she'd opted for the "holiday seating," which meant that the kitchen table had been carried into the dining room and fitted to the longer table there so that the two formed the shape of a *T*. The whole had been laid with her very best china. He wished that for once the good dishes had stayed in the hutch.

The Cutlers were solidly middle-class folk who lacked for nothing and wanted for little, but their lives seemed embarrassingly rich to Vince just then with all seventeen of them—Jolie made it eighteen—crowded around a table practically bowing beneath the weight of food. Obviously his sisters had pitched in even more than usual, and Jolie was looking a bit overwhelmed by it all. As if worried that she wasn't dressed well enough, she kept tugging on the hem of her simple white blouse, which she wore with black slacks and black loafers.

He pulled out a chair for Jolie and patted her arm in a gesture of encouragement. She didn't so much as glance at him but kept her gaze targeted on her lap. Bets howled about something, was gently scolded by both her parents and shushed by all her cousins, but then everyone settled into place.

His mother disappeared into the kitchen and quickly returned carrying two huge steaming bowls of hot biscuits draped with matching white dish towels. She placed one on each table and took her seat at the end of the top of the *T* opposite his father.

"Daddy, give us the blessing please."

Larry cleared his throat and bowed his salt-and-pepper head and delivered the requested prayer of thanksgiving. The rest of the family echoed his "Amen," and Vince squeezed Jolie's hands, realizing only then that he'd reached over to cover them where they were clamped together in her lap. He quickly withdrew his hand, hoping that no one else had noticed, only to catch several knowing smiles.

For some time, conversation was curtailed by getting everyone served. Eventually, however, the "interview" began. It would be, of course, Olivia who fired the opening volley.

"So, Jolie, where do you work?"

Vincent watched as casually as he could the very careful manner in which Jolie swallowed and laid aside her fork.

"Actually, she's doing some work for me," he blurted. "Laundry, decorating the house. I think I mentioned that when you came by the other day."

Jolie pressed her heavy linen napkin to her mouth and spoke.

"Mainly, I work for Geopp's Dry Cleaners."

"Oh, I know that place," Ovida said brightly. "I used to take our things there all the time, but I thought it closed down after sweet little Mrs. Geopp passed."

"Just for a couple of weeks," Jolie said softly.

"I'll have to start using them again, then."

"I'm sure Mr. Geopp would appreciate that."

It was Sharon's turn.

"Do you have family?"

Jolie toyed with her fork.

"An older brother and a younger sister. And a nephew."

"That's nice," Ovida gushed. "Do they live around here?"

"Yes, ma'am, but, um, we're not really very close."

"Oh, that's a shame."

Jolie hunched a shoulder in ambiguous reply.

"What do you do for the holidays?" Donna wanted to know, and again Jolie merely shrugged.

"Well, you'll just have to spend Thanksgiving with us," Ovida announced brightly.

Vince nearly choked on a hunk of steamed carrot.

"Oh, no," Jolie replied quickly. "I couldn't impose."

"As if one more will make a difference around here," Ovida said dismissively. "Now, I won't take no for an answer, seeing as how you have no other plans. Vincent, take a drink."

Vince croaked out a "Yes, ma'am," and gulped down half a glass of tea.

At least no one had asked about her parents. That was information which he preferred to impart privately. In fact, he should have done so before today. He wondered why he hadn't. Then he realized that he had wanted them to get to know her first, to *like* her first, not that they would hold her raising against her. He just wanted them to see her in the very best possible light.

This was getting a little scary. He couldn't remember another time when he'd felt this way about a woman.

The impulse to try to control the situation was very strong, so strong that he heard himself asking, "Have I told you how Jolie and I met?"

Of course, he hadn't, so he did so now.

"She leased my old apartment, and like a clunkhead I forgot to have my mail forwarded."

"I didn't know you got any mail there," Sharon said.

"Not much," he admitted.

"Not much!" Jolie yelped. "I'd accumulated a whole shopping bag full of his stuff before he finally came and got it. The post office and I played ring-around-the-rosy with it until I went to the library and looked up his phone number on the Internet."

Laughing stiltedly, Vince said, "Guess idiocy pays off sometimes." He caught Jolie's questioning glance and added, "You should see what she's done with the old place. That's what inspired me to have her help me out with my place. Why, if the apartment had looked that good when I lived there I might have stayed."

This brought groans and comments from all around the table.

"Took us ten years to get him out of there."

"And it still looked like a room in a frat house."

"At least he took down the pizza boxes."

"Yeah, how's that for decor? Pin empty, flattened pizza boxes all over the wall."

"I'm not sure he even scraped the cheese off first."

"Okay, all right," Vince objected, holding up both hands as if to fend off further comment. "The pizza boxes went the first year, and you know it."

"Then it was pages out of sports magazines."

"I wasn't even old enough to vote!"

"Hey, he could've gone to hamburger wrappers," Jolie quipped, and everyone laughed.

"So he's 'cooked' for you, has he?" Donna teased, crooking her fingers to indicate quotation marks.

Vince no longer tried to restrain his rolling eyes as everyone laughed at his expense.

"Y'all leave him alone," his mother scolded without the least heat before abruptly changing the subject. "So, Jolie, where do you go to church, hon?"

Jolie coughed behind her hand, smoothed that hand over the napkin in her lap and mumbled, "I, um, haven't been in awhile."

Vince felt a welling of unreasonable panic and didn't even realize that he was going to speak until he opened his mouth. "Her brother's a preacher, though."

Jolie shot him a look that lanced straight into his heart.

"Is that so?" his mother gushed avidly.

With a strained smile, Jolie said softly, "He has a small church in Pantego."

Ovida Cutler literally beamed. "How interesting. What kind of church is it?"

"What difference does it make?" Vince asked quickly, picking up his fork. Almost at the same time, Jolie answered, so that they talked over one another.

"You're right," Ovida said with a smile. "What difference does it make?"

Vince knew from the gleam in her eye that she was pleased. Jolie, on the other hand, was not, and he couldn't blame her. He wondered all over again what he was doing—and how likely he was to get in trouble by doing it.

All in all, dinner was a trial, but somehow they made it through. Jolie insisted on helping clean up afterward, which caused Vince some uncomfortable moments. He resisted the urge to follow her into the kitchen and run interference for her with the Cutler women, but just barely.

It seemed he need not have worried, however, for when they all trooped back into the den, where the guys were watching television, they were chatting like old friends. Then Jolie retrieved the folder of papers that she'd left with her purse and invited his sisters and mother to take a look at what she'd accomplished so far with his house.

They all exclaimed over the prices she'd given for the furniture.

"That's amazing!"

Jolie beamed, assuring them, "It isn't junk, either."

"Well, of course not," Ovida said. "Vincent wouldn't settle for junk."

"Oh, right, like that ratty piece of horsehair he's been sitting on all these years isn't junk," Olivia said.

"That was Grandma Sledge's sofa," Vince pointed out.

"Sentimental junk then," Sharon retorted.

"Oh, dear," Jolie worried aloud, "does that mean we shouldn't get rid of it?"

"No!" his sisters all exclaimed in unison.

"It really should be retired," Ovida agreed, and they all laughed. Vince took himself off to the safe company of the menfolk.

Some time later he realized that Jolie and his sister Donna had put their heads together for a fairly lengthy discussion, and once more his protective instincts stirred, but when he wandered over to ask what was up, Donna smiled secretively and answered only, "Girl talk, big brother, girl talk."

He knew too well what that meant, as did every other male in the room, but just in case he'd missed it, John translated for him.

"In other words, it's none of your business."

Vince did not agree, but he figured it was best not to probe too deeply at that moment. He'd survived this harebrained scheme so far by the skin of his teeth, but he was well aware that it could blow up in his face at any moment, which was nothing less than he deserved, frankly. Once he figured out what the dickens he was doing, he'd have some confessions to make, not to mention some apologies. Until then, he might just do best to keep his mouth shut, and thereby keep his head attached firmly to his shoulders.

He hoped.

Chapter Eight

Later, driving Jolie home at twilight, Vince figured that it was safe to ask what she'd thought of his family.

"Oh, they're great," she replied easily, "and your sisters and mom actually seemed to like what we're doing with the house."

He nodded, surprised but pleased about that himself.

"So what were you and Donna talking about for so long?"

Jolie smiled enigmatically, and he resigned himself to disappointment on that score, but then she said, "Decorating, of course. What else?"

He snorted at that. "I can think of a few dozen subjects I'd just as soon she didn't bring up, frankly."

Jolie laughed. "She just wanted to know what sort of furniture she could find at the market where you and I shopped."

"And?"

"And I expect that she and Martin will be spending some time in downtown Dallas next weekend."

It was his turn to laugh.

"Remind me to rub it in when Marty's griping about her buying new furniture."

She tilted her head to one side.

"Don't you like your brother-in-law?"

"Love him like a brother. I actually introduced him to my sister."

"Really? Just so you can irritate each other?"

He grinned. "It's a guy thing."

She arched an eyebrow but said nothing else, which was just as well, because he felt keenly the need to broach another subject. Shifting in his seat, he decided how to phrase it.

"I know it's none of my business, but I can't help wondering what's going on with you and your family."

Her eyes frosted, and she lifted her chin. "You're right. It is none of your business."

Like that was going to stop him, he thought, amazed at himself.

"I was just wondering if there was anything I could do to help. Family is important, and you seem so sad when you talk about yours."

Her gaze dropped to her lap, and she muttered, "There isn't anything you can do, believe me."

He was prepared to let it drop after that. What he wasn't prepared for, even after she turned her gaze out her side window and fussed with her bangs, was the tears that streamed down her face when she finally looked back to him. Instinctively he whipped the truck off the street and into the empty lot of a defunct car wash.

"Jolie?"

She shook her head, biting her lip. He slammed the transmission into Park, words tumbling out of his own mouth heedlessly.

"Honey, what's wrong?"

She gulped, and he leaned across the center console to wrap his arm around her shoulders.

"It's all right. Please don't cry."

"I c-can't help it," she finally whispered.

He brushed aside a strand of hair caught in the moisture on her cheek.

"I'm sorry. I didn't mean to make you cry."

"It's not you. It's…my life."

"Won't you tell me about it? You can talk to me, you know. I mean, we're friends now, aren't we?"

"I suppose we are."

She blinked and dabbed at her eyes with the edge of her sleeve. He scrambled in the console for a tissue and came up with a creased paper napkin.

"Thank you." She sniffed and pressed the napkin to her cheeks. After a moment she sighed and let her hands fall to her lap. "I told you that my nephew's father is in prison," she began softly. "What I didn't tell you is that my sister went to prison, too."

Vince rocked, knocked back by this revelation.

"Oh, man."

"They got her for abetting a crime," Jolie went on, "but Connie's always sworn that she didn't know what her boyfriend was doing when he went in to rob that bank branch, and she did turn him in when she heard on the news that he'd shot a guard."

"Well, that's good," Vince murmured, wanting desperately to say something positive, though he felt completely out of his depth here. Prison, for pity's sake.

"The guard was an off-duty police officer," Jolie went on, "and he died, so they sentenced her to five to eight years, but she actually served less than two."

"Sounds like she behaved herself."

"Model prisoner, they said." Her voice dwindled away with the next words. "That's why they gave Russell back to her."

Jolie choked and began to sob.

Russell? Vince's mind was whirling. Obviously he didn't have the full story yet, but all he could think to do at the moment was to wrap his arms around her and croon sympathetically.

"I'm so sorry. I really hate to hear this. I—I mean, I'm glad that she did well, but…you've obviously been though a great deal."

About the time he ran out of comforting words, Jolie calmed, turning her face into the hollow of his shoulder.

"I knew you'd understand."

Understanding had not yet been achieved, actually, but he didn't say so. Instead, he opted to ask the question uppermost in his mind, "Who, um, is Russell?"

That set her off again, and he could've kicked himself—except he still didn't know what it was all about. He figured all he could do was wait out the tears, and eventually she gulped, wiped and pulled in a shuddering breath.

"Russell is my n-nephew."

Her nephew. So that's why they'd given Russell to her sister; the sister was his mother. Vince sighed, pretty sure that he knew now where this was going, and already his heart was breaking for her.

"You took him, didn't you? While she was in prison."

Jolie nodded, blinking rapidly.

"C-Connie found out she was pregnant not long after she went in, and e-everyone thought it would be best if the baby was with f-family." She pulled in a deep breath and went on more calmly. "So I got certified as a foster parent and found us a little house. The state gives you a monthly stipend, you know. It was enough for two bedrooms and a little yard." She closed her eyes as if remembering. "He was perfect, just perfect. We were so happy, the two of us." Her hands plucked at the damp napkin. "Then just before Connie got out, my brother came to see me." She shrugged. "I didn't think anything of it. We saw him often."

"What happened?" Vince asked.

She closed her eyes and pinched the bridge of her nose. "He wanted to talk about Connie and Russell, about reuniting them. I couldn't believe it!"

Vince tightened the loop of his arms about her, feeling torn. On one hand, he couldn't argue against reuniting a parent and child, provided there was no history of abuse. On the other hand, Jolie had evidently cared for that boy for over a year, presumably from his birth. Did no one consider her feelings or what was best for her? Had no one prepared her for the day that the child's mother would reclaim him? However it had happened, it was plain that Jolie had been terribly hurt.

"So your brother helped your sister take back the boy," Vince surmised, and she nodded miserably.

"I guess I should have expected it, but the case-worker was always talking about *if* Connie could re-claim the child, and it just didn't make sense to me that she could go to prison and come out somehow a better parent than *me!*"

Vincent laid his head against hers, feeling her pain and the neediness that she tried so hard to keep hidden behind that tough-cookie mask of hers. Maybe she'd set herself up for disappointment, but that didn't make her grief any less real or poignant. Plus, she'd done a very good thing, caring for her nephew for at least the first year of his life. It must seem grossly unfair to be paid back with such a loss.

"I'm so sorry," he said against her temple. "And I'm sure you *are* a wonderful parent."

"You've no idea how much I miss him," she whispered, leaning into Vince. "I just couldn't believe they'd take him away."

"I guess there was a hearing?"

She nodded, becoming animated. "And Marcus testified on Connie's behalf," she said bitterly. "He talked about her 'spiritual maturity' and how she took parenting classes and college courses. He even let her and Russell move in with him! What hurt most of all was when he said that he feared it would be 'unhealthy' for Russell to be left in my care."

That, Vince could not imagine, and he was almost shocked by how easy it was to feel outraged on her behalf.

"Pure nonsense. Surely he didn't mean it the way it sounds."

"Maybe not," Jolie conceded, "but that doesn't change the fact that Russell is with them now, and I'm alone again."

Again. What a wealth of information and meaning that one little word contained.

"You are not alone," he protested automatically, tilting her face toward his with a finger curled beneath her chin.

"I've always been alone," she whispered, and he saw by the tortured look in her eyes that she really believed that.

"God never allows His children to walk through this world alone," Vince assured her, believing it wholeheartedly.

He'd once heard Hell described as complete and utter separation from God, and he shuddered to think of an eternity spent bereft of the slightest nuance of love. Somehow he understood that Jolie had felt too little love in her lifetime and too much separation.

Could he convince her that he wasn't going anywhere? Should he even try? Any words he might have given her to that effect seemed abrupt and premature, so he did the only thing he could think of to show her that he wanted to be a part of her life. He lifted one hand and cradled her cheek.

The impulse to kiss her shook him right to the marrow of his bones, but he subdued it.

Even as she drew away, color staining her cheeks, he understood that he was taking a big risk by opening himself up to the possibility that they could be more than friends. They were from very different backgrounds, and she did not seem able to trust. Yet.

She had issues to be resolved and wounds to heal, and he suspected that it would take a lot of patience and some very deft handling on his part to get them both to the place where they would have to be for anything more than simple friendship. But he couldn't ignore what he was feeling.

"I can't believe I told you all that," Jolie said with a grimace. "I hate it when people feel sorry for me."

"I don't feel sorry for you," he corrected firmly. "I feel sorry for what you've been though."

She smiled softly. "How is it that you always say the right thing?"

"We both know better than that," he said, "but if I got it right this time, I'm glad. In fact, I thank God."

She blinked and looked down shyly. He watched her pull together her usual bravado, enjoying every instant of the transformation. She was plucky, this woman. *His* woman?

Maybe. In time.

She fluffed her bangs and nervously smoothed them again, saying, "I'd better get home."

He took the hint and leisurely settled back behind the wheel.

He'd see her tomorrow, after all, and as often thereafter as he could manage until they both understood, individually and together, everything that God had in store for them.

Jolie had finally gotten a handle on the ever-plentiful laundry, so they were able to spend Monday afternoon shifting around the newly delivered furniture until everything was placed just right.

Vince was delighted to see that Jolie had been absolutely correct about the living-room stuff, and he told her so, which made her loft her eyebrows practically into her hairline.

"Frankly, I'm not sure which one of us is more surprised," she admitted, and suddenly he found himself slinging an arm around her shoulders as they both laughed.

Then she looked up at him, and he caught his breath as awareness sizzled in the air. Before he could figure out what he should do about it, she had whirled away, ducking down slightly to extricate herself from the loop of his arm.

"About Thanksgiving," she said, glancing away.

He reached for a nonchalance that he couldn't quite find and asked, "What about it?"

"I don't think I should come."

He caught his frown before it fully developed. "Why not?"

She shrugged. "Your family could get the wrong idea about us."

"My family's had the wrong idea since my sisters first walked in and found you here."

"Have you tried to tell them different?" she asked pointedly.

He wouldn't lie to her. "No."

"How come?"

"I don't know." He laid a hand against the nape of his neck. "You've met them. Do you figure it would do any good?"

She looked him square in the eye. "Probably not."

"Well, then, what's the point?"

She bit her lip. "I don't want to mislead anyone."

"Neither do I."

"So I'd better not come," she said decisively. Yet, he heard the faintest note of question in her tone.

He looked down at the toes of his boots and said baldly, "I want you to come."

"Oh?" She sounded a teensy bit hopeful.

He stuffed his hands into his back pockets and nodded. "I couldn't enjoy myself knowing you were sitting home alone at holiday time."

"No?"

"Not a bit."

She seemed to consider. Then, she shook her head. "It's not your problem."

"What's that got to do with it?" he wanted to know. "You'll still be alone, and I'll still be thinking about that instead of enjoying myself."

She rolled her eyes, and he scuffed a toe on the carpet.

"Unless there's a chance you might join your own family, after all."

"No chance of that," she stated flatly, folding her arms, "and I told Marcus so."

Vince felt a jolt of shock. "You mean he invited you to join them?"

She lifted her chin. "Surely, you don't think I could!"

He didn't know what he thought at the moment, but if she was determined not to join her own family, she'd just have to make do with his because he really couldn't enjoy Thanksgiving knowing that she was sitting out the holiday alone. He pulled out the big guns.

"Mom will be awfully disappointed if you don't come, you know, and how am I supposed to explain your absence? Saying that you can't abide being mistaken for my girlfriend would go over big."

She threw up her hands, as if it was all a great inconvenience, and exclaimed, "Well, I guess I'd better come then!"

He bit back a smile, sensing that her capitulation was less onerous than she pretended. "I guess so."

"I certainly wouldn't want to offend your mama after she's been so kind to me."

"Thanks," he drawled wryly. She didn't seem to have any qualms about offending him, but he'd take what he could get at this point. "Well, that's settled then. I'll pick you up about ten o'clock Thursday morning, if that's okay. Mom says we'll eat as close to noon as possible, but she likes everyone to be there early."

Jolie muttered something about sleeping in, but she nodded her agreement and left soon after, almost running to her car.

He chuckled about it, but later he sat in his special deerhide chair and thought about her or, more to the point, his feelings for her and whether or not he was supposed even to have them.

Looking around at the changes she had already wrought in his home, he tried to decide whether or not God meant her for him, or if he was supposed to somehow help her settle her differences with her family. Apparently they were willing, or at least the brother was.

Maybe that was all there was to it.

Or maybe this was about mutual need. Maybe she was just someone who could literally help him get his house in order, and maybe he was just someone who could fix her old car.

And maybe he would never know why God had brought her into his life.

All he could do was pray for guidance and trust that understanding would come when it was meant to—and that he wouldn't do something stupid like getting his heart broken in the meantime.

Jolie set down the iron and sighed, wiping her brow. She was beginning to hate ironing with a passion. Iron, iron, iron, that was all she seemed to do. That and laundry and planning designs in her head and shopping and arranging and…daydreaming about Vince Cutler.

In the beginning she hadn't wanted anything more than simple friendship from him, if that. Truth be told, she'd have settled quite happily for a cordial working relationship, but somehow one thing had led to another and before she'd known it, they were friends. From there, one short step had brought her to the possibility that they might be more to each other, which was ludicrous.

For one thing, she didn't want anyone in her life. Caring for people just got you hurt. She'd learned that all too well. For another, she was not the sort for Vincent Cutler. Vince came from a nice, normal family. He would definitely want a nice, normal girl, and that sure wasn't her, not with her background and her baggage.

Disgusted with herself for even briefly entertaining the idea that she might be more to Vince than a charity case, she turned her back on the ironing board and went to the sink for a cool drink of water. The outside temperatures were in the low forties, but in this tiny apartment standing over a hot iron, the air felt downright sultry.

So why did she feel cold inside?

She didn't have to look far for a convenient answer.

It was all Marcus's and Connie's fault. They'd used her and then betrayed her. They'd let her take care of Russell and then taken him away from her.

How could Vince even think that she'd accept an invitation to spend the holiday with them?

Wandering over to the counter, she picked up an envelope. Twice now she'd started to peel back the flap, and twice she'd stopped, telling herself that she didn't care what was inside. She'd recognized the handwriting on the front immediately. God knew that she and Connie had corresponded often enough in the past two years for her to know her sister's handwriting at a glance. She should have dropped the envelope in the trash the moment she'd realized who had sent it. Instead, she ripped the back flap off completely.

The card inside slipped out easily into her hand. The front was embellished with a cross and a white dove bearing an olive branch, symbols of peace and forgiveness. As if she had anything to be forgiven for, she thought resentfully, flipping the card open.

The verse printed inside was a quotation from Genesis 31:49. "May the Lord watch between you and me when we are absent one from another."

Jolie thought of her little sister's big green eyes and elfin face, and a lump rose in her throat. Willfully, she pictured Russell's bright coppery head and beaming smile, and the lump turned bitter. Quickly, dismissively, she scanned the short message that her sister had written.

It was all about how Connie missed her and wished they could have a "real family Thanksgiving." She asked Jolie to call her and wrote how sorry she was for "the misunderstanding between us." Some misunderstanding, Jolie thought disdainfully. She had been used, plain and simple, by her own sister. And brother. She wouldn't forget his part in it. They had used her and then cast her aside.

Even knowing that, however, she'd gladly do it all over again, just for Russell's sake. Even knowing that she would eventually have to give him up, she could never have walked away from the fat, cherubic little bundle who had been placed in her arms that day. Only hours old, he'd squinted and blinked at the bright world, pushing his tiny pink tongue against his lips hopefully, and she had instantly wanted for him all that she had missed: a stable and loving home, healthy meals, safety, laughter, a true sense of belonging.

She had tried so hard to give him those things, and

he had been happy, so happy. Did he miss her? she wondered wistfully. She loved him enough to hope that he didn't, and yet her heart cracked open a little wider at the thought that he might not.

Closing the card, she stuffed it back into the envelope and dropped it into a drawer. Out of sight, out of mind.

Please, God, she prayed silently. *I just can't bear to think about it.*

Then she remembered that God did not answer her prayers. If He did, she'd still be chasing Russell around on the floor, removing dangerous objects from his reach, rocking him to sleep, playing giggling games of peek-a-boo.

Emptiness overwhelmed her.

In the silence she heard the faint click of the thermostat kicking off or on inside the iron as it attempted to regulate the temperature of the pressing plate. Jolie gulped and swiftly moved back to the ironing board and the work at hand, desperate for anything that would take her mind off Russell.

She concentrated on placing and ironing the next garment, on getting the lay of a lace applique just right. Her hands moved by rote, and her mind wandered to something more challenging. The kitchen in Vince's house was bare and bland. He needed some attractive but useful items to scatter about the place. She tried to remember what he had, what he could use. She remembered the sandwich he'd made for her, the easy way in which he'd leapt up onto the counter to eat his share, the way his gaze moved over her face from time to time.

The slight dilation of his irises as he'd leaned close,

his hand warm against her cheek, his arm about her shoulders.

With a jerk she realized that she was fantasizing again about that moment in his truck on Sunday evening when it had seemed that he might kiss her. Just as it had then, her heart beat a rapid staccato inside her chest and heat rose up all the way to her cheeks.

What was she doing?

She already knew that she was not the sort for Vincent Cutler. No man was the sort for her. Any man whom she might want would never really want her, and she would not be like her mother, constantly used and tossed aside. She'd had enough of that already. She wouldn't be foolish enough to open herself up to more. Never would she wind up like her mom or even Connie.

Never would she have a child of her own.

Russell had been her one chance at real family, at motherhood. Without him she had nothing, not even the brother and sister to whom she had clung for so many years, despite the separation of different foster homes.

She was alone in the world, but at least she was safe from the pain of loving and losing.

Still, if she didn't have the Cutlers to spend Thanksgiving with this year, she wasn't sure how she would make it through the holiday.

The Lord never allows His children to walk through this world alone.

The Lord watch between you and me while we are absent one from another.

"Please, God," she whispered, "just this once. I can't go on thinking about them anymore. Isn't it enough that

I've lost my family? Can't I please just have some peace now?"

God, it seemed, was just not on her side.

Chapter Nine

"Evening."

"I see you're ready to shop," she said wryly, looking pointedly at his uniform as she slipped through the door of his house.

It was easier than looking at his face. Staring at that handsome face was much too dangerous. Besides, for some reason he looked especially inviting with a five o'clock shadow, very virile. Steady, she told herself. Vincent Cutler was just another guy, nicer than most, maybe, but in the end as much trouble as all the rest of them.

He shifted his feet self-consciously. "Look, I got held up at work. The drapery shop closes at seven, and I've got prayer meeting tomorrow evening, and with Thanksgiving being the next day, it's either tonight or wait until next week to check out this place, so I didn't take time to change. Do you mind?"

She rolled her eyes. The uniform was rumpled but clean and neater than her work clothes, which consisted of an old T-shirt and jeans worn to a pale gray-blue.

"I'm just teasing, okay?"

He lifted his brows at her tart tone but made no rejoinder.

"We'd better get a move on," he said, shepherding her through the house toward the garage. "It's not far, which is why I asked you to meet me here."

"And how did you hear about this place, again?"

"The fellow who built this house for me brought his car in for repairs today, and it occurred to me that he might have a lead on a good drapery place, so I asked him for a recommendation."

She nodded as he handed her up into the truck.

Not forty minutes later, she was climbing back into it, thoroughly disgusted. "And we thought the first place was high!"

"They *were* on the expensive side," he agreed, sliding behind the steering wheel. "Oh, well, nothing ventured, nothing gained."

"Nothing gained is right," she grumbled, buckling her safety belt. How dare that builder waste their time like this? she fumed silently. He probably knew what Vince was worth and figured he could afford such ridiculous prices. "Probably getting a kickback or something," she muttered, folding her arms.

Vince slid her a glance but said nothing. They drove back to his place in silence. Thankfully, it was a short trip. Jolie hopped down out of the truck and let herself into the house before he had the brake set. He caught up with her in the foyer, halting her progress toward the front door with a hand clasped around hers.

"Whoa," he said, drawing her around to face him. "Now why don't you tell me what's really bothering you?"

In the space of four weeks—and it was four weeks to the day, she realized with a jolt—he had somehow learned to read her like a book. Moreover, she seemed powerless to stop him.

"You're in a snit, and it's got nothing to do with overpriced drapery."

"I am not in a snit!" she defended hotly, but then she caught the concern in his gaze and gave up. "Oh, all right. I'm in a lousy mood, and I admit it. Happy?"

"Not until you tell me why."

She sighed gustily, but she told him. "I got a card in the mail from my sister Connie yesterday."

"I see." He led her into the living room, not releasing her hand until they were seated side by side on the couch. "What did she say?"

Jolie dropped her gaze, her fingers smoothing over the supple leather at her side.

"Not much. She's sorry for our 'misunderstanding,' like she didn't know taking Russell away from me would break my heart."

He didn't exactly rush to condemn her sister's actions. "Is that it?"

Jolie swallowed, feeling petty and frankly irritated about it. What had happened to her was *not* petty, but he was right to think there was more. "She wants me to call her."

"Are you going to?"

"No! Of course not!"

"How do you know it's not about Russell?" he asked softly.

Folding her arms, Jolie reluctantly told him, "She says that she wants a 'real family Thanksgiving.' As if we've ever had such a thing."

"Maybe it's time to start."

Her gaze zipped to his face. "How can we possibly? Connie and Marcus took Russell away from me!"

"And this might be a way for you to have him back in your life," Vince argued gently.

She couldn't believe what she was hearing.

"For moments here and there? I don't think so. It would be like losing him all over again every time we parted!"

Vince placed a comforting hand on her shoulder. "Don't you want to know if he's well and happy? Wouldn't it *help* to know that he's well and happy?"

She hungered for even the tiniest detail about Russell, but every thought of him still brought pain. Far worse, however, was the worry.

"And what if he isn't well and happy?" she whispered.

"Then you go to bat for him again," Vince said placidly. "You contact his caseworker, report what you've seen…"

She'd started shaking her head as soon as he mentioned the caseworker.

"They won't do anything! It would mean admitting that they were wrong."

"You don't know that."

"I can't do it!" Jolie leapt to her feet and began to pace. "I can't put myself through that again. You don't know what it's like to love a child and lose him, to finally be part of a family and have it ripped away! I'm better off alone."

He came to his feet beside her and stopped her in her tracks, his hands clamping her upper arms.

"You are not alone. You have never been alone. You never will be alone."

She cut him a scathingly skeptical look. "You're a great guy, Vince. You're kind and generous and caring, but I haven't lived the kind of life that you have. I didn't have model parents and a stable home. I didn't have a home, period!"

Dropping his hands from her shoulders, he said, "Maybe not, but that doesn't mean you were alone. You had your brother and sister, didn't you?"

"So what? I don't have them now, and don't try to tell me that it could be any other way, not after what they did to me!"

"What about God, Jolie?" he asked. "God is our constant companion. He's always there, always here. You just have to reach out to Him."

She could tell that, like Marcus, Vince was utterly sincere, and she wanted to be contemptuous about his beliefs, but she couldn't. Instead, she found herself being honest.

"Don't you think I've reached out? If God is here for me, Vince, then why did He let me lose Russell?"

"I don't know, honey," Vince admitted, "but I have to believe that He has a reason, a plan, and I know that God cares for you. I can prove it."

She was shocked by how much she wanted him to do just that, so much that when he led her back to the couch and gently seated her, she did not resist. Sitting down next to her, he wrapped an arm around her shoulders and bowed his head. Without even thinking, she bowed her own.

"Gracious Lord God, please help Jolie feel Your presence. I know how much You love her, but she's in so much pain that she can't feel it. She needs the peace and healing that come from truly knowing how much

You love her. It's so easy to lose sight of that fact when we're hurting, but no one can understand her pain better than You can, and no one but You can heal her heart. Please help her to see, to feel, that she's not alone. Help her to accept that she is loved, truly, deeply, constantly loved. Amen."

As he prayed, Jolie felt a warmth flow through her, and for a moment, just a moment, she did believe. Then doubt reared its ugly head.

She told herself that the warmth she felt was nothing more than Vincent's arm and her own wishful thinking. Trusting in God's presence and care would just leave her open to more disappointment because she wasn't the sort whom God could love, not *personally*.

She wasn't even the sort a mother could love—or a man like Vince.

She didn't say so. Instead she smiled limply, thanked him and said that she had to be going. Vince didn't argue, but she saw the disappointment in his eyes.

"I'll pick you up tomorrow morning at ten," he reminded her solemnly.

She smiled and flicked her hair off her shoulders with a toss of her head. "Sure."

How long would it be, she wondered as she left him, before Vince cut her loose just like everyone else in her life had done?

"Hold on there, scamp!" Vince snagged his nephew Matthew by the collar of his shirt and hauled him to a stop. "I'm pretty sure I heard your mom tell you to stop running in the house."

Matthew turned up his freckled snub of a nose and regarded his uncle with impish defiance. "Nuh-uh."

"Oh, right," Vince said, bending to bring himself muzzle-to-muzzle with the little miscreant. "That was *me*."

Matthew giggled uncertainly, his mind processing the backhanded order. When he had reached the obvious and only safe conclusion, he sobered conspicuously.

"Okay, Uncle Vince."

Vince smiled and straightened, patting the boy on the head.

"Good choice. Spread the word. The next one I catch running in here is going to be the *last* one to the table."

Matthew's face registered horror, and he went off at a fast walk to deliver the edict. Vince glimpsed Jolie hovering uncertainly just inside the kitchen door, where his mother and sisters churned around like marbles in a blender.

Jolie had been all smiles that morning, as if she couldn't be bothered to spare a thought for her estranged sister and brother or her absent nephew, but Vince knew that wasn't the case. He'd prayed long and hard about the situation the evening before, and he'd come to the conclusion that until Jolie made peace with her family, she wouldn't be able to trust anyone else. And he wanted her trust, wanted it very much.

Matthew's mother exited the maelstrom with a plate of deviled eggs. On the way to the dining room she patted Vince's cheek and teased, "Practicing to be a parent, are we?"

"Chapter and verse, son," his dad called over his shoulder from the easy chair in the den, his gaze never leaving the fuzzy picture on the old television set. "You've got to read 'em chapter and verse."

"For all the good it'll do," Matthew's father, Drew, said dryly. The other brothers-in-law had gone out front to look over a neighbor's new boat.

Vince changed the subject. "Hey, did I tell y'all that I've decided to get me one of those new big-screen TVs?"

"Excellent," his father said, glancing in his direction. "Super Bowl party's at your house this year. But aren't those sets pretty expensive?"

Vince shrugged. "Jolie's saved me a bunch of money on the house decorating, but I'm still shopping around. I figured I'd better do it while I'm in a spending frame of mind."

Abruptly Drew bolted upright on the couch and hooted, pumping his fist in the air while Larry flopped back in his chair and groaned. Vince switched his attention to the television, becoming aware at the same instant of a presence at his side.

"What happened?" Jolie asked, looking to the set.

Controlling his surprise, Vince answered calmly, "Drew's team scored." Jolie wrinkled her nose, and he laughed. "What? You don't like them?"

"They've got the lamest uniforms in the NFL," she complained. "Just look at that logo. I know what it's supposed to be, and I still can't identify it."

"That's no reason to dislike a team," Drew protested.

"Yeah, well, their quarterback's got a shallow draft," Jolie went on knowledgeably. "He falls back only two steps, and then he does this double-pump thing that totally alerts the defense to his target." She shook her head and added, "He'll run out of stunt plays soon, and then the other team will clean his clock for him, I don't care how good his line is." With that she turned back into the kitchen.

Vince blinked, aware that his brother-in-law and his father were staring at him with mouths slightly ajar. It had taken concerted effort and drastic measures to get his sisters even minimally interested in live football, and they still wouldn't watch more than five minutes of a televised game. His mother had no interest either, and in her case nothing seemed to make a difference, not tickets to a pro game, not autographed photos, not detailed explanations. Jolie, on the other hand, came already programmed. Vince grinned and shrugged at his father and brother-in-law, letting them know that he was as surprised as they were.

Drew shook his head as if to say that it wasn't fair. Then a roar from the television yanked them all back into the game. It was Larry's turn to hoot.

"Hey, Jolie!" he crowed. "The game's tied! Ran it all the way back from the kick-off!"

She popped her head out of the kitchen in time to catch the replay. Afterward she dismissed the play with a dry comment.

"Lucky break. Special teams have been sputtering all season."

Vince and Drew laughed at the look of consternation on Larry's face.

As soon as she disappeared again, Larry looked at Vince and admitted softly, "Too bad she's right."

"I heard that," Jolie informed them loudly.

Larry ducked his head, grinning as everyone else laughed.

Vince privately marveled. Who'd have guessed that she could fit in like this? He leaned back against the wall and perked up his ears, wondering how it was going in the kitchen with the female half of the clan.

As usual, they all seemed to be talking at once, but he heard Donna say, "Mmm, Jolie, these potatoes are good. What'd you put in them?"

"A little broth. Cuts back on the fat."

"Don't let Dad hear you say that," Olivia counseled wryly.

"It's Thanksgiving," Sharon said, mimicking their father's voice. "It's a feast. We're *supposed* to eat fat."

"And do we ever!" Helen chortled.

"They're yellow enough. He'll never know the difference," their mother said. "Somebody turn up the oven. These rolls are almost ready to go in."

"I'll do it," Donna volunteered. Vince heard the screech of chair legs against the floor and pictured his heavily pregnant sister hauling herself up out of the seat into which she had dropped earlier, complaining of a backache.

Just then a blood-curdling scream erupted from the closed-in back porch where the kids were playing. Olivia somehow recognized the voice of her youngest and yelled, "Michael?"

Drew popped up onto his feet, announcing loudly, "I'll go." He headed toward the back of the house. "Michael? Matthew? Mark? What's going on out there?"

Content that Jolie was holding her own for now, Vince wandered over and dropped down onto the end of the sofa that Drew had just vacated. His dad leaned forward, propped his elbows on his knees and jerked a head toward the kitchen.

"So what's her story then?"

Vince didn't pretend to misunderstand him. He'd been prepared for this question. He gave out the capsulized version.

"So she's not close to her brother and sister," Larry surmised correctly. They were much alike, father and son, not only in build and coloring, but in attitude, too.

"Actually, they're estranged," Vince admitted, still very troubled by that. "Long story short, for various reasons Jolie wound up taking care of her nephew for the first year or so of his life. Then a few months ago, her sister took the boy back and their brother helped her do it."

"That's tough." Larry shook his head sorrowfully.

"The thing is, she can't seem to come to terms with it."

Larry clucked his tongue. "Well, give her some time, son. I know women as well as any man can, and I figure she's dealing with a real sense of loss and betrayal right now. Those are especially big issues for women, and given what you've told me, it must be even more difficult for her than most."

"Yeah, I suspect you're right there."

He worried that if she didn't soon find peace with her situation and form some reconciliation with her family she would grow even more angry and resentful than she already was. She'd close herself off entirely then, and he didn't want that. He just didn't know what to do about it. God could and would help her accept, forgive and conquer her pain, if only she was willing to let Him. Getting her back in church seemed to be a logical first step in the right direction, but she'd already refused one invitation to attend with him.

Lord, how do I reach her? he prayed silently.

Before he could follow that thought, his mother rushed into the room, a dripping ladle in one hand, a wild look in her eyes.

"Larry, get the car!"

"What?" His father twisted around in his chair.

Ovida didn't answer him. Instead she abruptly addressed Vince. "Get Marty in here. Now!"

Vince stood, still not sure what was going on, and caught the murmur of concerned voices in the other room. He glanced through the doorway, straight into Jolie's pale face, and suddenly he knew.

Bolting for the front door, he heard his mother's exclamation. "Her water broke!"

Forget the turkey, they were having a baby!

Jolie stood with her mouth open like some spectator at a train wreck.

It was pandemonium, with the women cramming food into the refrigerator and shouting out instructions to one another, the men zipping around in the background, and the kids crowding around the kitchen door to stare at the laboring mother as if expecting the baby to burst from her belly like some alien in a horror movie.

The only calm one of them, Donna herself, was right at the center of the storm. Despite her white lips, guttural moans and roiling belly, she managed to sit patiently, smile and work her way down a mental checklist while her family careened around like Keystone Kops in a panicked attempt to shut down dinner preparations and get her to the hospital.

"My suitcase is all packed and sitting inside the closet door," she said to no one in particular. "The doctor's telephone number is programmed into Marty's cell phone. All I've had to eat is a hard-boiled egg and crackers. There's a list of people to call on my bedside table."

She looked right at Jolie, who couldn't seem to do more than gape, as she said that last. Then she reached out, sucking in a sharp breath at the same time. Instinctively, Jolie wrapped her fingers around Donna's and squeezed.

Sinkingly aware of the others rushing from the room, she asked, "Are you all right?"

Panting, Donna nodded, gulped and gripped Jolie's hand even tighter. "St-strike the family names from the list," she instructed. "That'll leave the church and two others. Vince can make those calls after we get to the hospital. Okay?"

"Uh-huh."

Marty skidded through the doorway into the dated but homey kitchen, Vince on his heels. He went down onto his knees at Donna's side, demanding, "What's wrong?"

"Nothing."

"B-but Vince said—"

"I'm having a baby," Donna snapped. "It's perfectly normal."

"But it's not due yet!"

"Tell that to the baby!" She grimaced at his look of worry and added softly, "A month early is nothing to worry about. Everything will be fine."

He placed his hand on her belly and fervently said, "From your lips to God's ears."

Stepping up behind Jolie, Vince cleared his throat and said, "John's sedan is waiting out front." His hands settled gently upon Jolie's shoulders, and she fought the most astonishing urge to lean back against him.

"Who's behind the wheel?" Marty asked anxiously.

"Dad."

Martin shook his head. "No, no, he's too slow. You're the wheel man. I want you."

Donna rolled her eyes as Vince flexed his hands on Jolie's shoulders. "No problem," he said mildly. "Let's go."

Donna tugged on Jolie's hand as she began pushing her way up out of the chair. Bracing herself, Jolie helped haul her up, Marty hovering solicitously at his wife's side.

"Mom sent Sharon for a clean robe for me to wear, and Helen's gone for towels," Donna said, plucking at her wet clothes. Jolie blinked. She'd missed those details entirely.

"Let's head for the door," Vince said, stepping back to make way. "Mom and Olivia are herding the kids into Wally's van."

"Oh, I can stay here with the kids," Jolie offered, glad to have something to contribute.

Donna just laughed. Vince squeezed her shoulders again.

"Thanks, hon, but it would take a battalion of armed soldiers to make that work. The Cutler clan descends en masse for every family event."

"Just hang on," Donna instructed. "They'll need every hand at the hospital."

"Oh, no," Martin moaned. "I think I'm going to be sick."

"For Pete's sake, Marty," Donna chided, her free hand on her belly as he hurried away. "Make it quick, will you?" She lifted her arm. "Vince, lend a hand."

He slid to her side, wrapped an arm around her back, murmuring, "I've got you, sis."

"Nothing new there," she muttered and kissed his cheek.

The trio sidled through the door, Jolie taking up a position on Donna's other side. Helen rushed past with the towels, shouting, "John, put Bets in the car with us. Vince and Jolie are going with Donna."

"Tell Dad I'm driving," Vince called out as she disappeared through the front door.

"Good grief, Marty," they heard her say. "Could you do that in the grass?"

Donna moaned, then she laughed. "Poor Martin. You be nice to him, Vincent Cutler, or I'll pull your ears off your head."

"Me?"

"Don't pretend you won't tease him," Donna scolded.

"Never occurred to me." Vince winked at Jolie over the top of his sister's head, and a smile quirked her lips. The next instant she was blinking back tears.

Jolie couldn't help thinking about Connie going into labor all alone and in a hostile place instead of surrounded by loving, teasing family. They were like nothing she'd ever known, these Cutlers. Donna was so fortunate, and Jolie sensed that she knew it and also that even now, in the midst of happy crisis, she was doing her best to make Jolie feel included.

Sharon met them at the front door with a black bathrobe.

"Here you go, sugar. This won't show stains."

"Isn't this Dad's?" Donna asked, pausing to shove her arms into the wide sleeves.

"He never wears it," Sharon told her dismissively, "so don't you worry about it. Where's Marty?"

"Throwing up on the lawn," Vince answered smugly.

Sharon laughed, and to Jolie's surprise, Donna sniffed and a tear rolled down her nose.

"He loves us so much," she said in a happy, shaky voice, rubbing her belly.

"Of course he does," Vince said solicitously, shoving open the screen door. "Here we go."

What would it be like, Jolie wondered enviously, to feel such love?

She stuck to Donna's side as they again negotiated a doorway.

It was chilly in the shade of the porch, but the sun shone brightly overhead despite the clouds scudding along pushed by a brisk wind. An ashen Marty wore a jacket draped about his shoulders, and Sharon's husband Wally was busily dispensing coats to everyone else.

"Over here," Vince called, holding out one hand. "The corduroy and the denim."

"And the fur," Sharon added, striding forward to receive all three coats. She draped the bronze-colored faux fur around Donna, did the same for Jolie with the ivory corduroy walking coat and tossed Vince his denim jacket as they drew up at the car. Larry was waiting with the rear door open and the motor running.

"Marty, you go around," Donna said, presenting her cheek for her father's kiss. "Vince is going to drive, Daddy."

"Whatever you want, doll." He went around her and got in on the passenger side.

Donna ducked down and carefully edged into the car, the seat of which was lined with towels.

"We're right behind you," Sharon promised, moving toward another vehicle.

Jolie hung back hesitantly, until Vince placed a hand at the nape of her neck. She looked up at him, and he dropped a smile on her, saying, "Let's go, sweetheart. Hurry."

Sweetheart. Once or twice he'd called her honey or hon, but sweetheart seemed so…so…*romantic*.

Gulping, Jolie slid in next to Donna, who immediately gripped her hand again, despite the supporting arm that Marty had wrapped around her shoulders. Vince quickly swung down behind the steering wheel, reaching for his safety belt.

"Okay, let's get this show on the road."

"Owww," Donna moaned as the car backed out of the drive.

"Isn't this happening too fast?" Marty asked Jolie worriedly. Before she could formulate an answer for that, Larry reached into the back seat and covered Donna's and Jolie's linked hands and began praying aloud for a safe delivery and a healthy mother and child.

The other family members echoed his "Amen." Then Donna gasped and dropped her head onto her husband's shoulder.

"Let's move it!" Martin ordered, suddenly taking charge. Vince flicked on the hazard lights, pressed down on the horn and gunned the engine through a yellow light at the corner.

Donna was going through her mental checklist again by the time they pulled up under the canopy at the hospital. It seemed to help her keep the pain at bay.

"Suitcase in the closet. List on the bedside table. Oh, and the vent in the baby's room should be opened. We want the nursery nice and warm when we get home."

"I'll take care of it," Marty promised, bailing out, but as he disappeared into the hospital, Donna turned to Jolie.

"Tell Sharon. She'll see it gets done."

"Sharon," Jolie promised. "A-and Vince is to call."

Marty reappeared with a nurse pushing a wheelchair. Larry got out and hurried around to the door that Marty had left open. Donna scooted forward, pausing long enough to pat her brother on the shoulder.

"Getting off easy, buddy, with all the family in one place."

"Yeah, considerate of you," Vince cracked, glancing into the rearview mirror. "Take care of yourself, sugar," he added as Donna slid awkwardly out of the car. "See you soon."

"Fifth floor," Marty informed them, closing the door as his wife settled into the wheelchair. Vince sighed and readjusted his mirror to meet Jolie's gaze.

"Never a dull moment," he quipped, and started the car forward again.

That, thought Jolie, was as gross an understatement as she'd ever heard. How very blessed the Cutlers were!

Chapter Ten

Vince found an empty spot and parked. His family members were already piling out of vehicles in other places as he opened the back door of the sedan for Jolie. She took his hand as she rose to her feet.

"Are you sure I should be here?" she asked uncertainly, eyeing the horde of Cutlers swarming toward the hospital.

He looked down at her, brushed a strand of hair from her cheek and clasped her hand tightly in his.

"Yeah," he said. "Yeah, you should."

Suddenly, Jolie knew that there was no other place in the world where she would rather be. Perhaps it was odd, but she felt welcome. The Cutlers had a way of doing that. They were probably like that with everyone, though, not just her. Still, she felt special, included.

"Why would you think you shouldn't be here with the rest of us?" Vince asked.

Jolie shrugged. "It just seems odd." A heartbeat later she softly and unexpectedly added, "I wasn't there when Russell was born."

Out of the blue, longing stabbed her, so sharp that it felt like a knife between her ribs. One moment she was fine, and the next she'd have given her last breath to see Russ. And Connie, Marcus, all of them. How she missed them!

Despite all that had happened, she missed her brother and sister. How weird was that?

Vince slipped his arm around her and turned her to follow the others at a rather sedate pace, telling her, "You were there when it counted most."

"I guess so," she murmured uncertainly.

"You did a good thing with your nephew, Jolie," he told her firmly, "and I'm sorry you got hurt because of it, but it grieves me that you aren't at peace with your family. Won't you consider seeing them, trying again?"

Her heart swelled painfully at his gentle words, but then it contracted with fear.

"I'd just be letting myself in for more heartache," she said tremulously.

Vince dropped his arm and strolled at her side, silent for the moment.

"It's a risk, I admit, but isn't the possibility of mending the rift worth it?"

He couldn't understand how it would be, how it had always been for her and her brother and sister.

"Vince, you have a big, wonderful family. You can't know how much I envy you. But the Wheelers aren't like the Cutlers. Our parents were never there for us, and we kids haven't really been close since Child Welfare split us up."

"What about before that?"

"Before that," she echoed, remembering with sudden clarity.

She didn't even realize that she'd come to a halt as the images and sensations flowed over her.

Connie had been little more than a baby with her pale, wispy locks and frequently trembling chin. Jolie remembered the urgent strength in her thin, ropy arms as they'd banded about her, seeking solace and reassurance. Only two years older, in many ways Jolie had felt responsible for her sister. Unfortunately as Connie had grown and matured into a very beautiful girl, she had continually reminded Jolie that she was not *that* much older, the implication being that she was not that much wiser and shouldn't give advice.

Marcus had been an avenging angel during their childhood. How fierce he had been! When the other kids had made fun of their mismatched clothing and perpetually runny noses, he had lifted his chin and pressed back his shoulders and stared them down with fists clenched. Every time their mother disappeared he'd solemnly taken over the task of caring for his sisters, and Jolie had believed that he could do no wrong.

With adulthood, his thick hair had warmed to a light, toasty brown which just missed blond. His solemn green eyes no longer seemed overly large for his face, a face that had been too thin and rawboned for a boy. He had changed in other ways, too. He was calmer, more confident. How calmly he had stated his case against her and devastated her world!

In retrospect, she realized that it wasn't the first time. Their world had come apart the day that Marcus had gone next door to beg food from the neighbors.

With the gas cut off and no groceries, they'd had to force down macaroni without cooking it. The bread had been growing blue stuff, but they'd eaten it anyway. Finally, all they'd had left was a mushy piece of tomato. Marcus had said what they'd all known, that their mother was not coming back, but Jolie couldn't believe it when he'd said that he couldn't take care of them anymore.

Rage swamped her all over again at the memory of it.

Strong, hard hands closed around her upper arms.

"You're trembling."

Jolie shook off the difficult memories, saying automatically, "It seems to have gotten cooler."

"Let's get inside." He linked his fingers with hers and tugged her toward the brown brick building.

"Are you sure I won't be in the way?" she asked again, dragging her feet.

Surely she didn't belong with these nice, normal people.

"Hey, what's one more when it comes to the Cutlers?" Vince replied teasingly.

"Remind me to ask the nurses that," Jolie retorted, giving back as good as she got and falling into step beside him.

Vincent grinned. "They're probably shuddering to see us coming. It's not the first time this has happened, you understand."

"Obviously."

"And it won't be the last," he added, squeezing her hand.

Jolie's heart fluttered, and she dared not even wonder why. All she knew was that she'd somehow gotten swept up in the Cutler universe and, oddly enough, that she liked it. She didn't know how that had happened, but she did know that it couldn't last.

Nothing good ever did, not for her. But at least she was a small part of something normal and happy now. She supposed that was as good as it was going to get.

"Oh, man, look at that, will you?"

Vince pressed his palms against the glass partition between the waiting area and the nursery. His newest nephew lay screaming, tiny limbs flailing beneath the taut blue blanket, his face a jowly mask of pasty red flesh below a tiny, white knit cap.

Beside him, Jolie stood very still, her hands splayed against the glass partition. Vince could feel the ache in her. He knew that she was remembering her nephew as a newborn, and his heart went out to her.

She cleared her throat and commented in a voice that was almost normal, "Your dad says they're going to name him Anthony."

"Anthony Martin," Marty confirmed proudly, coming through the door that he'd been popping in and out of for almost five hours now. He hadn't stopped beaming since he'd first given them the news.

"How's the new mama doing?" Larry wanted to know.

"Mad as hops," Marty announced happily. "Doc's told her that she has to stay flat on her back for several hours when she wants to be up rocking the little squaller in there. Ovida's making sure she stays put for now."

"She'll be praying for somebody to keep her down this time next week," Olivia observed dryly.

"Hopefully it won't be too bad," Marty said, "My folks are on their way from Tulsa, and Mom's planning to stay a couple of weeks. You know how first-time grandparents are."

"God bless them," Sharon said with a nod, and that started a mild squabble about how she, as the oldest daughter, had gotten the lion's share of attention and assistance after giving birth to the firstborn grandchild on *both* sides of her family. In the midst of it, a nurse pecked on the nursery window.

"They're going to let me take him in to her again now that they've got him all cleaned up and charted," Marty said, disappearing once more through the door.

"That'll make mama happy," someone said.

A general silence descended. Then Drew suddenly asked, "Has anybody thought about the game?"

That brought several exclamations from around the room. Vince's was among them.

"Hey, that's right. It's just ten days away. Will Donna be able to go, do you think?"

"I wouldn't count on it," Helen answered.

"Doubtful, very doubtful," Olivia confirmed.

"Even if baby Tony had come on time, she was cutting it close," Sharon pointed out. "She told me that if she couldn't go they were planning to give her ticket away."

"Maybe Marty will take his dad in her place," someone said.

"He's declined in the past," Drew noted. "I think the only sport he cares for is golf."

"Well, Larry, looks like you'll get to be one of the sibs this year," Wally said, but the family patriarch shook his head.

"Naw, naw, that's a deal for the younger generation. I'll stay home with Mom as usual. Y'all take Jolie there. She's a football afficionado."

All eyes, save those of the children who were standing with their noses pressed to the nursery glass, turned to Vince and Jolie. It hadn't occurred to Vince even to mention this Cutler family tradition to Jolie, but the opportunity to include her suddenly seemed golden, for more reasons than one.

"What do you say, Jolie? Want to see a pro football game?"

"You're kidding."

He shook his head. "Not at all. We've been attending the first local game after Thanksgiving for years. Used to be just us guys, but gradually the girls got in on it, too."

She looked thunderstruck. "You're serious? A live pro game?"

"We buy the tickets at the beginning of every season," he confirmed. He was sure that Marty would be glad to let him take this year's extra off his hands.

"You're going to love it," Drew assured her, leaning back as best he could in his stiff, shallow chair.

Vince could tell from the look in Jolie's eye that she was afraid to get her hopes up.

"Don't worry," he said. "It's a week from this coming Sunday."

Her eyes brightened. A weeknight would have been problematic, but she didn't work on Mondays, at least not at her regular job. He could guarantee that her other "boss" would understand and be extremely flexible about starting times.

"Thing is," he went on mildly, "there are strings attached. The deal includes church."

"Church," she echoed uncertainly.

"Yeah, see, the timing's a little sticky so we'll all be attending early service together and leaving straight from there."

She nodded, biting her lip. "Uh-huh. Are you sure they haven't made other plans for the ticket?"

"No, I don't think so," Sharon said.

"I think Donna was holding out in hopes of making it herself," Helen said with a glance at her sister.

Sharon shrugged. "Maybe so."

"What do you say?" Vince asked Jolie. "Want to go?"

She took a deep breath—and smiled. "Sure! I'd love to go."

"Excellent."

Vince clapped his hands together and breathed a silent sigh of relief. He'd tried to get her to go to church before, but she'd resisted for one reason or another. He had sensed her ambivalence, even anger, though he doubted she would admit to it, and he could understand to a certain extent, since her brother was a minister. She had reason to be hurt, and he knew that the anger she was feeling directly resulted from her pain and loss. Unfortunately, he suspected that until she released the anger, the pain of her loss would not release her, and it seemed to him that the way to do that was to get her back into church. At least he hoped so.

Lord, let this be a first step in that direction, he silently prayed, even as the conversation continued.

"Wear flat shoes," Sharon warned her.

"And bring some warm pants," Helen added. "I always wear two pieces, like a sweater and a skirt. Then I just slip my pants on in the ladies' room after church, tuck the skirt into a bag, and I'm good."

"And don't forget your coat and scarf," Olivia warned. "The seats are about halfway up in the stadium, and it can get real chilly."

"Especially if the weather turns," Wally said, prompting a discussion about the year an errant wind had driven sleet through the hole in the roof of the stadium right into their faces.

The air was thick with jolly reminiscence by the time his mom stuck her head through that door and waved at his dad.

"Grandpa, get in here."

"About time," he exclaimed, getting to his feet.

"Wally and Sharon, you're next."

"I want to go!" Bets pleaded as Larry moved swiftly past her. "I want to hold the baby."

"Not today," Helen said flatly.

"Please, please, *pleeease.*"

"She can go in my place," John said, and that set up a wail from the other kids.

"Brenda can go in for me," Wally announced.

"Just let the girls go," Drew proposed.

"No way," Vince said. "I'm going in."

"What about you, Jolie?" Sharon asked. "You ought to get to go in."

Feeling her immediate withdrawal, Vince piped up again. "She'll stick with me."

"Oh, no, that's all right," she began, but he sensed that this was something she needed to do, whether she realized it or not.

Seizing her hand, he bent his head close to hers.

"Donna will expect it. You don't mind, do you?"

She gulped, and he prodded a little harder, keeping his voice low.

"I know it's difficult, but it would be a shame not to see this thing through to the end. Come on. He's just a little baby."

Finally she drew a deep breath and nodded uncertainly.

"That's my girl," he crooned, sliding an arm around her.

He realized as he said it that it was true, at least he'd like to make it true. Against all odds, Jolie Wheeler had somehow carved out a niche for herself in his life. She'd lodged herself in his heart, and he instinctively wanted to keep her there. Whether he could or not remained to be seen. Vince knew himself to be an all-or-nothing kind of guy, and he understood that the make-it-or-break-it point of any new relationship could be just around the bend, but there was no turning back now, not for him.

He draped his arm casually around her neck and drew her closer. It was something he might have done with his sisters, and she seemed to take it that way, but he let himself imagine what it could be like if she was his girl. Full of hope, he listened to his family's banter and held Jolie at his side where, God willing, he meant to keep her.

It was, no doubt, a mistake to hold little Anthony Martin, but when Ovida matter-of-factly dumped the impatiently fussing little guy into her arms, the weight of him felt so right cradled against her chest that Jolie hadn't possessed the strength to immediately pass him on. She thought of Russell and his sweet, placid nature.

How frightened she had been when he'd first been placed in her arms. Then she had looked into his blinking, unfocused eyes and fallen head over heels in love. She would never feel that again, never hold a child of her own. How could she when she was obviously meant to live her life alone?

They were a touchy-feely lot, the Cutlers, always hugging and kissing each other's cheeks, patting and holding hands, so she wasn't particularly surprised when Vince stepped up behind her and casually surrounded both her and the baby in a loose embrace. Looking over her shoulder, he cooed to the baby, who blinked his big, navy-blue eyes and stopped mewling long enough to listen to a voice other than his own.

Suddenly what she would be missing hit Jolie with the impact of a bullet fired at close range. She felt as if she was bleeding from the heart. It wasn't just Russell whom she was missing. It was all those children she would never have.

Unless…

She turned away from the temptation of that thought and gave up the baby to one of his aunts. When Vince patted her shoulder, she knew that he understood at least some of what she was feeling.

Somehow that made it even worse.

Friendship was one thing; a future was something else again. She must not let herself believe that she could have the kind of future for which Vincent Cutler was obviously destined. She was not meant for that kind of life; nothing in her experience had prepared her for it.

Sidestepping, she put her back to the wall as if making room in the crowded hospital suite. Vince folded his arms.

When Donna declared that she was too exhausted for company and that they all needed to get out so she and little Tony could rest, Jolie was secretly relieved. If she could have found a polite, subtle way of doing it, she'd have gone home, but when she hinted to Vince that she, too, was tired, he insisted that she couldn't skip the Thanksgiving meal even if it had been delayed.

They convoyed to the Cutler home, and everybody pitched in to reheat the food and get it on the table. The family seemed determined to make a great celebration, even without Donna, but Jolie's heart was no longer in it.

Marty stayed only long enough to gulp down a plate of food, and Jolie toyed with the idea of asking him to drop her off on his way back to the hospital, but his eagerness to return to his wife's side would not allow her to impose. Besides, she felt duty-bound to help with the clean-up.

Finally, Vince drove her home. When he casually inquired if she had plans for the weekend, she felt a spurt of annoyance. All she wanted at the moment was to be alone with her misery.

"What weekend?" she retorted, implying that she'd be working Friday and Saturday as usual. "If you mean Sunday, I intend to do nothing at all."

The truth was that Geopp had elected to shut down the business for a couple of days so he could visit with relatives in Louisiana. Ever since she'd learned of this unexpected holiday, she'd been wondering what she was going to do with herself. Now she only wanted to lock herself away until her defenses were shored up again.

One corner of Vince's mouth crooked upward in what could have been a grimace or a grin, but he said nothing more on the subject.

Relieved, Jolie told herself that she needed the time to rest. She felt emotionally and mentally drained. Indeed, by the time she climbed the stairs to the landing, she was practically asleep on her feet. She fell into bed and dreamed of infants wailing forlornly as she tore through hospital corridors searching for something she could never find.

She woke in the morning to despair. Her thoughts turned immediately to Russell and to Donna and baby Anthony. And to Connie and Marcus. And to Vince. And to everything else she had spent her life wanting and could never have.

Chapter Eleven

When the telephone rang on Saturday afternoon, Jolie's first thought was that it was Vince, but the caller ID revealed that the call originated from her brother Marcus's number. After a surprising moment of agonizing indecision, she let the machine get it and then erased the message without listening to it and turned off the telephone.

Why not? She had no more business talking to Vince than to her brother or sister. There was not a single person in the world that she must talk to, and it was better that way. A solitary life was safest, simplest, easiest. She didn't have to get her heart broken repeatedly to learn that lesson.

By Monday morning, she'd convinced herself that she wanted no deeper involvement with Vince Cutler than a casual friendship, which was as it should be. They had made a business deal that was mutually beneficial, and as honest people of good will, they had formed a friendly working relationship, nothing more. The dinner invitations with his family and the upcoming football game were incidental offshoots of their business relationship, and it would be beyond foolish to seek anything more. She resolved to keep her distance.

It should have been easy.

When she arrived at his house for work, he was dressed and ready to go out. That was fine by her. In fact, it was preferable to having him underfoot all day.

"I see you're ready to leave," she said airily, moving toward the kitchen and the laundry room beyond.

"Not me," he said, snagging her hand and drawing her to a halt. "We. Or have you forgotten about the drapes?"

She had. She'd forgotten everything after the events of Thanksgiving, everything but the laundry waiting for her. "I have work to do now."

"You sure do," he agreed, towing her toward the garage.

She dug in her heels. "First things first. Let me get the laundry done, then if there's time—"

"We'll make time," he insisted, bringing his hands to his hips. "The laundry can wait a little while. I'll help you with it later."

"It's *my* job," she reminded him sharply. "I'll do it."

He tilted his head, studying her. "Fine. Then you'll do it *later*."

Jolie set her back teeth, gritting out, "You're the boss," as she swept past him. What he said under his breath, she didn't catch, mostly because she didn't want to.

"You going to glower at me all day?" he asked, following her into the house after another unsuccessful shopping trip.

"I'm not glowering at you," she snapped. "I'm frustrated. Doesn't this town have a reasonable drapery supplier hidden away somewhere?"

"I don't think it's the store owners who are being unreasonable," he muttered.

She rounded on him. "That's a hateful thing to say! I'm only looking out for your best interests! You may like being cheated and ripped off. I don't!"

Irritation flared. "Face it, Jolie," he told her flatly. "The drapes are going to cost what they're going to cost. We've been to every shop in town. Pick one, and let's get this thing underway."

"You pick one!" she shot back. "It's your house." With that she whirled and flounced down the hallway to the laundry room.

He let her go, not trusting his own temper at the moment, and trudged into the kitchen. His intuition told him that something more than the obvious was going on here. She'd been stiff-arming him all day. Why didn't she just set up barricades and tattoo Do Not Touch on her forehead? So much for taking the next step toward a real relationship.

Rubbing his own forehead with the heel of his hand, he leaned against the counter and told himself that he shouldn't have backed off after Thanksgiving. At the time he'd thought he was giving her room to decompress after all the excitement of the baby coming early and the family reaction to it. On a normal day the Cutler crew could overwhelm a person, even him! A self-contained soul like Jolie didn't stand a chance. Obviously she'd used the weekend to reinforce that protective shell she'd built around herself. Now he'd have to chip another hole in it.

He bowed his head and asked God to show him what to say and how to say it. The answer was quick in coming. With a sigh, he turned and ambled into the laundry room. She was stuffing a load into the washer as if it was trying to escape.

"I'm sorry," he said to her back.

She froze for a moment, poked a few stray ends and bits into the tub and slowly shifted around to face him.

"I know you're doing your best for me," he went on, "and I know that it goes against your grain to pay more for something than you feel you should. I'm sorry I let my impatience get the better of me."

She gulped and turned her back on him again, busily dumping detergent into the washer and twisting dials.

"It's not your fault," she finally said without turning around. "I'm in a lousy mood. But you're right, I don't like paying more than I think I should. I don't like for *you* to pay more than I think you should, either. And don't bother saying that you can afford it. That's beside the point."

"Is that really what this is about?" he asked cautiously.

She turned, shrugged and leaned back against the washer, arms akimbo as she braced her hands on her hips. "What else?"

He let the possibilities percolate for a minute. "You get another letter from your sister?"

She immediately got busy cleaning out the lint trap in the dryer. "Nope."

He wasn't fooled. "Your brother?"

"No." But she hesitated first.

"One of them call or come by?"

She balled the lint into her fist, closed the dryer door and walked over to the trash can. "He might have called."

"Might have?" Vince echoed.

She dropped the ball of lint into the trash and then watched it lie there. "I saw his number on the caller ID."

"But you didn't talk to him."

He hadn't meant it to sound accusatory, but she evidently took it that way. After slitting a quick glance at him from the corner of her eye, she pinched the bridge of her nose.

"Look," he said, "I'm not spoiling for a fight. I understand the situation with your brother and sister. I'm just wondering what this mood of yours is really about."

"What mood? I don't know what you're talking about."

"I think you do. I think you know I like you. A lot."

She shot him a quick, sharp look, too quick for him to tell if it was astonishment or dismay.

"Well, I—I should hope so."

"And I think you like me, too," he forged on.

"Of course." She said it lightly.

He wasn't fooled. "I think you like me a lot," he went on doggedly, "a lot more than you want to."

She turned to face him again. "That's ridiculous."

He had her now. "Oh, good." He rocked back on his heels. "Then there's no reason you won't go to dinner with me Thursday night."

She blinked. "Uh."

"You're not busy Thursday night, are you?"

"Uh."

"Friends do that, you know, have dinner together."

Her lips flattened. "Friends. Right."

"Excellent! I'll pick you up about six-thirty, give you time to change after work."

"We can talk about the drapes," she said emphatically, obviously trying to set boundaries.

"Right," he said, grinning. With that, he walked away and left her to her work.

They could talk about anything they wanted to talk about, anything at all, the weather, the economy, philosophy. They'd talk about whatever pleased her, but they would be talking as more than mere friends this time. Of that he had no doubt.

Jolie feared that he'd drag her off to a showy, upscale restaurant and spent hours trying to figure out what to wear. In the end she chose a pair of black jeans faded to charcoal gray and a simple burnt-orange turtleneck. It wasn't fancy, but it was the best she could do.

Vince showed up in jeans, complimented her looks with a casual comment and took her to a popular chain restaurant serving Mexican food.

After ordering, they talked about what sort of drapes she had in mind for the house and what they were obviously going to cost. Jolie had accepted the fact that the draperies were going to cost more than she'd like. After that, it had been a relatively simple matter to decide which of the custom drapers should get the work. Vince approved her choice and suggested that they make an appointment to revisit the shop on Monday. Jolie agreed, and he said he'd take care of it.

When the food came, he prayed over it as usual, but this time he took her hand before he did so. Jolie felt compelled to bow her head alongside him. She really had nothing against speaking a blessing over her meal, and she could admit privately now that a part of her previous reaction to his habit had been aimed, not at him or the act of praying, but at her brother.

Sometimes it seemed that she could not escape Marcus or reminders of him no matter what she did. She'd see a pair who looked similar in appearance and wonder if they were brother and sister. Even children, who were easier to identify as siblings, caused her a pang because she couldn't help remembering how close she and Marcus and Connie had once been.

It was no different that night. As soon as she lifted her head after the prayer, Jolie came eyeball-to-eyeball with a little girl sitting next to her older brother in a booth across the way. The child smiled, rattling her appetizer plate against the tabletop, and the boy calmly dropped more tortilla chips on it without interrupting the parents' conversation. Jolie had to look away.

Only when she pulled her attention back to her own table did she realize that Vince still held her hand in his. He gave her a sympathetic look and squeezed her fingers. Quickly she smoothed her napkin in her lap, requiring both hands to do so. It disturbed her that he seemed able to read her thoughts so easily, but she couldn't deny, even to herself, that his concern left her with a warm feeling.

Despite her best intentions, she found herself relaxing, and that made conversation flow more easily. Soon they were bantering and teasing like...well, like the friends they were. The food disappeared, and the check was settled, and yet they lingered at the table, talking and laughing—until the little girl and her family across the way rose and began to leave the restaurant.

Jolie couldn't help glancing at them one more time,

and that prompted Vince to say, "You must miss them. I know I'd sure miss my sisters if something happened to drive a wedge between us."

She didn't pretend to misunderstand.

"I do miss my brother and sister, but this is not some silly childhood argument. Frankly, I've never been so hurt or disappointed in anyone."

He nodded and changed the subject, sort of.

"One day when you have your own children, you can use this to help them value their relationship and get along."

Jolie opened her mouth to say that she would never have children of her own. She'd have to fall in love and get married before that could happen, and she had no intention of letting herself get that close to anyone. Still, she couldn't seem to force out the words. She told herself that it was because he would almost assuredly try to talk her out of her decision to remain alone, but the truth was that saying it aloud felt too much like making it real.

She settled for an inarticulate, "Mmmm," smiled and said, "We probably ought to go and free up the table."

He nodded, rose and held her chair while she slipped out of it. Then he helped her with her coat and escorted her from the building. She tried to recapture the mood, but she kept thinking of what he'd said about using her experiences as a parenting tool. That made a certain sense—for a person planning to make a family, a person whose experience had taught her that family was not for her.

Before he dropped her off at her apartment building, he reminded her that the football game was coming up on Sunday and that she would need to be ready by eight o'clock in the morning. She assured him that she wouldn't forget, and assured herself that Sunday would be about fun and friendship only.

She awakened early after yet another restless night. Marcus had called the afternoon before and left another message. She'd stood there and listened as he'd spoken to her answering machine, but she hadn't picked up the telephone, telling herself that there was no point in doing so. If she hadn't slept well, she chalked it up to the excitement of attending a pro game.

Never in her wildest dreams had she ever imagined that she would do such a thing, but then much about her life seemed beyond her imagination. That thought pre-occupied her throughout the morning, so that when Vince knocked on her door, she was in an agony of indecision, despite having thought she'd resolved the issue of what to wear.

"Does this sweater go with this skirt?" she demanded of him anxiously.

He answered automatically. "Sure."

Irritated and impatient, she stomped a foot, brought her hands to her waist and demanded, "Look at me! I'm trying to figure out what to wear."

He let his gaze wander from her feet upward. By the time it got to her face, he was smiling. "No, I guess the sweater does not go with the skirt, after all."

She threw up her hands and whirled away, snapping, "Why didn't you say so?"

He just chuckled as she hurried into the bathroom to change the sweater for a simple, tailored blouse which would work well with the double-breasted navy wool coat that she'd picked up at the military surplus store.

It was hard to justify spending good money on a fashionable winter coat in Texas, but she did her best to dress up the outfit with a wooly scarf. After stuffing knit gloves into her pockets, she took one last look in the mirror, adjusted the dark-blue knitted headband that she wore to keep her hair out of her face, fluffed her bangs and went out. Vince was standing exactly where she'd left him, his hands in the pockets of his brown corduroy jacket.

"I'm ready."

"You look terrific," he told her. "Stop worrying."

She rolled her eyes. "I'm not worrying, but thank you."

"You're welcome. Shall we?"

He offered her his arm. She linked hers with it and went out to embrace what she hoped would be a redletter day.

She didn't expect church to be the highlight of the outing. Feeling betrayed, Jolie had stopped going to church when Marcus had first broached the subject of returning Russell to his mother. She'd told herself that if God didn't care enough about her to keep Russell with her where he belonged, then God didn't care whether she was in church or not. Ever since she'd accepted Vince's invitation, however, she'd secretly felt a certain relief.

As it turned out, Vince's church provided an eyeopening experience. For one thing, Vincent Cutler, good as he looked, good as he was, couldn't carry a tune in a bucket. She, however, could.

Jolie had always enjoyed singing along with the radio, and Russell had seemed to like her voice well enough, but she'd learned to love singing hymns at

Marcus's small church. Vince's church was quite large, large enough to boast a hundred-voice choir and a state-of-the-art sound system, with a large video screen that showed the words to each song. Given the season, the place was packed, even for the early service, and all those voices lifting heavenward in praise made her feel as if she might float right up to the ceiling.

"We usually sit down there on the right near the front," Helen had whispered before the service had begun. She'd pointed over the balcony rail. "The pastor likes to leave the back seats for visitors. You know, so they don't have to go searching for an empty spot in a strange place. That's him there."

When the hymn-singing portion of the service had concluded, the pastor stepped up to the pulpit, bade the congregation rise for prayer and read off a list of names of those in need. Next he read a list of those with praises. When he mentioned that Donna, Marty and the new baby were home and well, he waved up to the balcony, and quite a number of heads turned to smile and offer silent congratulations to the family. Most of those seemed to take note of Jolie standing beside Vince.

As if in answer to a collective question, Vince took her hand in his, so that they stood side by side, hand in hand, with heads bowed throughout a long but eloquent and obviously heartfelt prayer.

Once they sat down again, a quartet provided special music. Jolie couldn't imagine hearing better vocals. At the end of the selection, the pastor returned to the pulpit and placed his burgundy Bible atop it. After instructing them to turn to the twenty-fifth psalm, he began to read in a strong, dramatic voice.

Jolie hadn't remembered to bring the Bible that Marcus had given her for Christmas some years earlier, but Vince leaned forward slightly and laid his own Bible in her lap, open to the correct passage. He lifted one arm about her shoulders and with the other hand pointed out where they were. She took the Bible into her hands, and her eye picked up on the fourth verse.

"Make me know Thy ways, O Lord. Teach me Thy paths. Lead me in Thy truth and teach me, for Thou art the God of my salvation. For Thee I wait all the day. Remember, O Lord, Thy compassion and Thy loving kindnesses, for they have been from of old. Do not remember the sins of my youth or my transgressions. According to Thy loving kindness remember Thou me, for Thy goodness' sake, O Lord."

The preacher looked up and asked a simple question. "Have you asked God to teach you His ways?"

Jolie felt a thunk, as if something had dropped from her chest into the pit of her belly. She forgot about Vince's arm draped casually about her shoulders and let the preacher's words fill her.

"If not, why not?" he went on. "Our God is the God of salvation, the God of compassion, a loving, kind God who forgets, just wipes out, our sins and transgression, all for the asking. 'Well, pastor,' you say, 'if I ask to know God, He's going to expect something of me.' I don't deny it. On the other hand, friend, if you ask to know God, He's going to *make* something of you."

Jolie listened, fascinated, and what the pastor had to say made a lot of sense. This was very different from what she had experienced from time to time as a child, when church had seemed a confusing, often boring, kind of punishment, and from what she'd known at Marcus's church. As his sister, she'd often been more concerned with how others saw and heard him than with the contents of his sermons or how they might apply to her.

She wondered with a pang if she had been unfair to Marcus. He had often urged her to consider the words that he delivered from the pulpit, but she'd had a difficult time doing so. He was her brother, not some oracle from God. She'd been proud of him, but she hadn't wanted to take his sermons seriously. Why not?

The answer came in a blinding flash of insight, and suddenly she found herself caught up in a maelstrom of emotion. Tears welled into her eyes, and even as she listened to the pastor with suddenly sharp ears, she came to a clear and abrupt understanding of herself. She hadn't listened to Marcus because she'd already been angry with him.

"Some of you don't want to know God," the preacher was saying, "because you don't want to know yourselves. You want to maintain your illusions. You think you've got the world and yourselves figured out. Knowing the maker of both would just confuse things, throw your little make-believe world into a tailspin. Well, make-believe is a prison, ladies and gentlemen. Always remember that the truth is what sets us free."

The truth was that even before Marcus had sided with their sister and taken Russell from her, Jolie had been angry with him. Deep down, she'd been angry with him for years. Ever since the day Child Welfare had arrived to cart them off to foster care, she and Connie to one home, Marcus to another, Jolie had been bitterly angry with her brother.

He had gone to the neighbors. He had abdicated his place as their protector and caretaker. Her heroic, solemn, big brother had turned out to be only a boy, after all. The protracted absence of their mother had given him no choice, really, but at the time it had seemed to Jolie to be the ultimate betrayal. She'd known it was unreasonable even then, and perhaps that was why she was only just now facing that anger.

"You push God away," the preacher was saying. "He's reaching out to you, but you keep pushing Him away with your indifference and your defensiveness and your cynicism and your wrath. This world isn't perfect, so you label God a tyrant, unfair, uncaring. 'What's He ever done for me?' you say. It's a very long list, but I'm going to give you a one-word answer that says it all. Jesus."

Jolie shuddered with something she couldn't describe, not an emotion really but a knowing, an opening. It left her feeling shaken and vulnerable, and suddenly she yearned with a startling ferociousness for her brother. She heard his voice inside her head just as she'd heard it on the answering machine the previous day.

"Hello, Jo," he had said, sounding sad and wistful. "Hope you're well. We're all fine. Russ is growing like a weed, really running around the place now. You did good by him, Jo, he's a happy, loving little boy. We were wondering, Connie and I, what your plans are for Christmas. We missed you Thanksgiving, but we prayed that you didn't spend it alone. Every day I pray that you'll pick up the phone and call. Please, Jolie, let's be a family again. Please think about it."

She did think about it. For a moment, she could see

and feel it so clearly, how it had been to be a real family. Then she realized that everyone was getting to their feet. They sang another hymn, and she managed to go through the motions, but she was too distracted by thoughts of her brother, sister and nephew to make sense of the words. She felt as if she were reeling, and she reached mechanically for the old pain and resentment, anything to steady herself.

Surely, she told herself petulantly, Russell missed her as much as she missed him. How could Marcus say that he was fine? How could any of them be fine after all that had happened?

And how could they ever be a family again? Too many years and too much hurt had gone by since they had been a real family. Maybe if they hadn't grown up in different foster homes, maybe if Connie hadn't gone to prison, if they hadn't teamed up to take Russell away from her after she'd stepped in to care for him, if her mother had just once thought of her children instead of the latest man to whisper promises in her ear…

"You okay, hon?"

The sound of Vince's voice jolted her. "Huh?" She looked around to find that the building was quickly emptying.

"The girls are going to change for the game. Did you want to go with them?"

"Yes!"

She grabbed her bag and turned to follow Helen along the curving row of seats and out into the crowded aisle, aware of Vince watching her, his hands at his waist. She dared not look back. Everything seemed to have bobbed to the surface, all the hurt and anger and longing that she'd suppressed all these years, and if he saw her face, he would undoubtedly know.

Following along in Helen's wake, Jolie carefully tucked away all her mental and emotional corks, but something told her that it would only be a temporary fix at best.

Chapter Twelve

Inside a stall in a surprisingly opulent ladies' room, Jolie changed into her jeans. The sisters did the same, chattering about Donna's Thanksgiving baby and how little sleep the new mother had gotten since they'd come home from the hospital. Several others had crowded into the small space, and Sharon made a few introductions, but Jolie knew that she'd never remember who was who despite the friendly smiles and speculative looks.

Finally the foursome hurried out to greet the men, throwing on their coats. Sharon and Olivia seemed especially enthusiastic about the game. Helen, who was the quietest of all the sisters, seemed to be missing Donna. She and her husband John automatically fell into step beside Vince and Jolie, who suddenly realized that Marty was missing, too.

"Is Marty meeting us there?" she asked as they pushed out onto the sidewalk.

John shook his head, and Vince said, "Guess he didn't want to leave Donna and the baby. He called this morning and told us to give his ticket away."

"Give it away!"

"Sure, why not?" Vince asked, taking her hand as they crossed the traffic lane and moved toward the parking lot. "If he's not going to use it, somebody else might as well."

"He's not going to try to sell it or anything?"

"Scalping is illegal," John said matter-of-factly.

"Technically," Wally added over his shoulder. "There are ways around that."

"Yeah, and one of them is to give the ticket away," Vince said. "Marty says he has too much to be thankful for to worry about missing a game and losing a few bucks."

"I think it's a nice thing to do," Helen put in. "Why don't we all pitch in and pay him for it, then we'll each have a part of giving it away?"

"That's a good idea," Olivia agreed, turning around to walk backward as they made for her minivan. "If each couple gave just twenty-five dollars, that would leave Marty and Donna with an equal stake. Then we'd all be giving away the ticket."

Everyone agreed to that, everyone but Jolie who stopped dead in her tracks, gaping at the thought of a ticket that cost a hundred and twenty-five bucks! It took everyone a moment to realize that she wasn't with them, then they all stopped and Vince walked back to ask, "What's the matter?"

"Who paid for my ticket?" she wanted to know.

She hadn't really thought about it before. Somehow, though, she'd assumed that the family had bought the tickets together and that they'd cost maybe thirty or forty dollars each, which seemed like a lot to her. Three or four times more seemed outrageous, and she couldn't let Donna and Marty give that kind of money to her!

Vince reached out and fingered the lapels of her coat, stepping close.

"Better face the facts, Wheeler," he told her softly. "I paid for your ticket because you're my date." He stepped closer still, bringing his forehead near hers and staring down into her eyes. "It's better than letting Marty take the hit for two tickets he couldn't use, isn't it?"

His date. A couple. How on earth, she wondered wildly, had this happened? She shook her head, thoroughly confused, but then his face clouded and she found herself nodding. Vigorously. He grinned and grabbed her hand, turning back to the others and dragging her along with him.

"What are you waiting for?" he asked loudly. "We've got a game to go to!"

That seemed to light a fire. Wally pumped his fist, and the whole group piled enthusiastically into the van. Jolie and Vince crammed into the back seat with Helen and John, leaving Sharon and Wally to the shorter middle one and Olivia and Drew to the front buckets. Vince sat on the outside edge, crossing his legs and extending his feet out into the space between the shorter middle seat and the van's sliding side door.

On their way to the stadium and while inching forward into the parking lot, they talked enthusiastically, the men dissecting the opposition, the women anticipating the food and the people. Sharon and Helen entertained Jolie with stories about fan hijinks, and it became clear to her that they watched the crowd more than the players. They all talked over one another, joking and laughing and generally just having a good time.

That laid the pattern for the remainder of the day. After hiking in from the "back forty" as Drew called the parking area to which their seats entitled them, they gave Marty's ticket to a grateful young couple who traded the seat in for a cheaper one and used the difference to pay for a second. After making their way to the seats, the women shed their coats and handbags and announced that they were going for food. Vince crammed bills into Jolie's hand and asked for nachos, sausages (plural), a burrito, a large soda and a dill pickle, adding that she should get herself anything she wanted.

She looked at the money in her hand and wondered if he expected her to order filet mignons, then she got a look at the actual prices and wondered who in his right mind would spend that kind of money for junk food! The Cutlers apparently, because the sisters loaded up, teasing one another about wearing the goodies on their hips as they made their way back to their seats.

"Good thing we only do this once a year," Helen remarked.

"Speak for yourself," Sharon quipped drolly. "You can look at my fat behind and know this isn't a rarity for me."

Sharon was pleasantly rounded, like her mother, but Jolie didn't think of her as "fat." The other girls, who took after their father, as did Vince, immediately protested the self-description, and by the time they rejoined the men, Sharon was prancing around like a beauty-pageant contestant, dipping and swirling comically.

As soon as the bounty was passed out, the group huddled together for a quick prayer, then settled into their seats just as the opposing team emerged from the locker room. Jolie had never felt quite so avid. Vince glanced at Jolie's single sausage on a bun and asked if that was all she was going to eat.

"It's not even lunchtime yet," she said.

"But it's game time!" Drew crowed, stuffing a dripping nacho into his mouth.

"Yeah, if you're going to hang out with this crew," Olivia said, leaning forward to peer around Vince, "you're going to have to learn to pig out."

"How else can you date our pig of a brother?" Sharon piped up. Jolie looked down. Was she dating Vince or was it all for show on his part? Just then Vince reached around Jolie to lightly smack his oldest sister in the back of the head just as she was about to bite into her hot dog. The result was chili on her chin and nose and a lot of laughter.

The home team burst onto the field just then, and the crowd rose to its feet, including the Cutler contingent. Vince took a napkin and cleaned Sharon's face for her. She stuck out her tongue at him, then darted around Jolie to kiss him on the cheek. Jolie couldn't help feeling a little envious of the easy, teasing camaraderie that the siblings and their spouses enjoyed.

She would never again have the same with her own brother and sister. *Unless I can somehow forgive,* she caught herself thinking. Immediately, she tried to push that thought away. How did she put away her hurt and anger?

The question stubbornly clung to the back of her mind throughout that long and amazing afternoon.

Vince slung an arm across Jolie's shoulders companionably as they strode toward his truck in the church parking lot. Behind them, Drew tooted the horn of the minivan as it turned onto the street. Lifting his free arm high in farewell, Vince gave in to the impulse to pull Jolie a little closer.

"So what do you think?"

"About the game?" she asked, smiling.

"The game, the crazy Cutlers…the service this morning."

"It was great, all of it," she replied sincerely.

Vince smiled. "So, what was your favorite part?"

She shook her head. "This whole day has been… words fail me."

She'd laughed with the rest of them all afternoon, and she'd really gotten into the game, making some astute judgment calls about various plays and rulings. She'd even loosened up enough to splurge on fajitas. Still, throughout the day he'd sensed that she was experiencing some sort of emotional turmoil. It could have been his imagination, of course, but he decided to go with his gut feeling.

"Want to talk about it?" he asked gently as they drew near his vehicle.

She stiffened, but her reply was flippant. "Sure. Let's see." She struck a pose, one arm folded across her body, one finger tapping her chin, as he fished out his keys and unlocked the passenger door. "We should not have lost that game," she concluded, climbing up into the seat.

Vince chuckled. He'd given her the perfect out. Next time he'd choose his words a little more carefully. After walking around the truck, he inserted himself behind the steering wheel, unsurprised when she took up right where she'd left off, rattling on and on about the game.

"The team's just too young, you know. Can't take the pressure."

Vince nodded agreement. Really, he couldn't quibble with her assessment, but that wasn't why he let her get away with dissecting the game play by pivotal play as he drove her home.

At one point he interrupted long enough to ask, "How'd you get so into football, anyway?"

"What else is there to do during football season? I mean, that's all that's on television Sunday afternoons and Monday nights."

"Which just happen to be your two days off from your regular job." And of course, she would not have cable, he added mentally, making her pretty much a captive audience of whatever stations she could pick up with a pair of rabbit ears.

"There you go," she confirmed matter-of-factly.

He smiled, thinking that he had unintentionally benefited from her straitened circumstances, while she launched into a story about Sharon's hips or some such thing. He wasn't really paying attention any longer. Instead, he was weighing the advisability of pressing her to reveal what was actually going on inside that pretty head of hers.

By the time they reached the apartment building, he'd concluded that no good cause would be served by letting the matter go. Sooner or later, she would have to deal with some of her issues—or he was going to have to reconcile himself to simple friendship with her, something he didn't want to contemplate. He sent up a silent prayer and shut off the engine.

"Can I come up? We need to talk."

She blinked at him, frowning slightly. "Sure."

Smiling to let her know that this didn't have to be a frightening conversation, he let himself out of the truck. She was already doing the same, so he waited for her to join him. Side by side, they headed for the stairs.

As they entered the apartment, she flipped on the lights and asked if he wanted something to drink, but he groaned at the very thought.

"I am stuffed. I won't have to eat or drink for at least two days."

She arched a censorial eyebrow, announcing airily, "I am not surprised."

Laughing, he said, "Come on, let's sit down."

He lifted a hand, but instead of putting hers in it, she turned toward the sofa and dropped down onto one end of it.

"What's wrong?"

He sat down next to her and calmly replied, "That's what I want to know."

She shook her head, gaze skittering away. "Not following."

Carefully considering his words, he folded his hands.

"There were moments today when you were somewhere else entirely, and I don't think it was a happy place."

She sighed and rubbed her hand through her bangs, muttering, "Nothing gets by you, does it?"

"Couldn't say. All I know is that I like to keep it real, especially between us, and when something's bothering you, well, seems that it bothers me, too." Surprisingly, tears sprang into her eyes, and without even thinking, he slid close and drew her into the circle of his arms. "Hey, now, it wasn't my intention to upset you."

She gave him a watery snort, insisting, "I'm not upset, I'm…confused."

"What about?"

She bowed her head, and for a moment they simply sat together. Finally, she spoke.

"It's almost too much, you and your family, me and my family, what the preacher said today."

He lifted his arms from about her and locked his hands, meshing his fingers.

"Let's start at the end and work backward. What exactly did the pastor say that's got you thinking?"

She spoke hesitantly at first and then with growing agitation. Who could really know God? Why would He forget the bad things we do? Vince answered her patiently and in some detail. Knowing God, he told her, was a lifelong process. One had to believe, of course, and then ask and keep on asking to know God's will. Most importantly, one had to pay careful attention to God's replies.

"As for forgetting our transgressions," he explained, "it pleases God to forget how those whom He loves hurt Him. Again, all that is ever necessary is that we ask for His forgiveness, and afterward He wipes out our sins as if they never existed."

Jolie admitted that she just didn't understand how that could be.

"Don't make the mistake of saddling God with our human weaknesses," he told her. "And understand now that His strength is also ours for the asking."

"But why?" she demanded.

He considered for a moment.

"Let me ask you a question. Don't you want to forget the pain?" Her eyes widened. "Our sin pains God, but He loves us, so why would He want to remember our sin?" Vince went on. "God *chooses* to forget, but before forgetting must come forgiveness. If you want to forget your pain, Jolie," Vince said, "first you have to forgive."

Her brow wrinkled, and she whispered, "I'm not sure I can. If it was rational, maybe, but…"

"If what was rational?" he asked. When she hesitated, he urged, "Tell me."

To his gratification, she trusted him with the story of her childhood, with the anger she had discovered only that day. Coupled with what she felt was her brother's betrayal in the matter of her nephew, the realization obviously rattled her. He listened until she had talked herself out, sometimes weeping, sometimes bitter, more often just plain hurt and confused. Afterward, they sat quietly, taking comfort in each other's company until the emotional storm had truly calmed and Vince felt that he could broach the last difficult issue.

"You know, this whole tangle might unsnarl itself if you'd just see your brother and sister."

"How can I do that?" she demanded, sitting up straighter. "How can I risk that kind of heartbreak again?"

Vince leaned forward, bracing his elbows on his knees.

"Doesn't it make a difference that you wouldn't be coping with it alone this time?" She blinked at him, and he saw immediately that she was as afraid to trust in that as in anything else. "No, of course, it doesn't," he answered himself.

He sat up again and turned slightly to face her, praying that what he was going to say was the right thing.

"Has it occurred to you that this isn't about you? You're hurt. All right, I understand why that is so, but what if this really is best for your nephew? What if knowing his mother loves him is more important than knowing that you love him? And why shouldn't he have both?"

For a long moment, she stared at him as if he'd sprouted horns. Then she shifted around until their knees touched. "Do you really believe that?"

"I don't know," Vince told her softly, "but I believe that God always has a reason for allowing what goes on in our lives, and it makes sense to me that Russell could only be better off for having a loving relationship with both his mother and his aunt."

"I want to forgive," she said after a moment, "but I don't know how."

Vince smiled and took her hands in his. "It starts with a prayer," he began.

They slipped to their knees, and Jolie poured out her heart, all her hurts and fears and failings. She begged God to help her forgive.

After a long while, they rose

"Thank you," she whispered to Vince, dabbing at her eyes with a tissue pulled from her pocket.

"My pleasure. I hope this means that you're willing to talk to your brother and sister now."

"Forgiving and opening yourself up to more hurt are two different things, Vince," she hedged uncertainly.

"Just think about it," he urged, "and while you're considering it, I'll be praying for you."

She nodded, half smiling. He saw a glimmer of trepidation in her eyes and knew that she had not yet conquered her fears. He understood instinctively that she must, but it was only as he drove himself home a little later that he realized why.

Not only did her happiness depend on it, but theirs together did as well.

And they *could* be happy together.

In fact, Vince was beginning to believe that they *should* be happy together. It seemed to him that God was blatantly leading them in that direction.

At least his heart seemed to think so.

Vince ran a fingertip around the rim of his cup and glanced up just as his father came through the door of the coffee shop. Waving, Vince snagged Larry's attention and sat back into the corner of the booth, one elbow propped atop the edge of the seat back. As he slid onto the bench opposite Vince, Larry turned up his coffee cup and signaled the waitress with a look.

"Cold out there," he commented, rubbing his hands together.

Vince noted that his father's fingers had grown knobby and stiff.

"Arthritis acting up?"

Larry nodded. "Yeah, that twenty-two-degree temperature drop last night kicked it up a notch."

"Well, that's Texas for you."

"You're telling me? I've seen it drop forty degrees in two hours and without a cloud in the sky."

"Blue norther," Vince recollected, but then he changed the subject. "I need your advice."

"Figured something like that," Larry said, pressing back in his seat as the waitress arrived with the coffeepot. She poured the steaming black liquid, ascertained that they didn't want anything else and departed again. "What is it then?" Larry asked, leaning forward to hunker around his cup. "Jolie?"

Vince smiled wryly. "How'd you know?"

"Well, it wouldn't be business. Nothing I can tell you

there. And if it was about the family, you'd be talking to your mother. So I figure it's got to be Jolie. You in love with her?"

Vince nodded matter-of-factly. "Yeah. Yeah, I am."

"How come?"

The blunt question momentarily shook Vince, and to his surprise he found himself growing angry.

"How come? What do you mean, how come? What's wrong with her?"

"I didn't say there was anything wrong with her."

"She's a little rough around the edges, okay?" Vince retorted defensively. "Who wouldn't be, given all she's been through. In fact, it's a wonder she's not selling herself on some street corner, but instead she's managed to maintain her dignity. She lives her life with a certain sense of honor, and if that makes her a little standoffish, then who are we to judge?" He pecked himself on the chest. "I've lived a life of pure bliss compared to her, and I know that if our roles were reversed I'd be the worst sort of thug. If you really want to know the truth, she's too good for me!"

Larry sat back with an air of satisfaction.

"Well, that answers that question. Now how about her? Is she in love with you, too?"

Rubbing the back of his neck, Vince ducked his head and admitted, "I don't know. I think she could be if she'd let herself."

"Trust issues," Larry commented mildly, lifting his cup. "Not surprising."

"Big trust issues," Vince confirmed morosely, "and it's all centered on her family. I know in my gut that if she can't patch it up with them, we can't go forward."

"What are you going to do?"

Vince toyed with the spoon on his saucer. "What would you think about me arranging a surprise meeting with Jolie and her brother and sister?"

Larry kept his eyes averted while he considered, but then he shook his head. "An emotional ambush isn't the answer, even if your motives are good. That would just make her mad at you."

Vince scowled and shoved a hand through his hair. "I wouldn't mind her being mad at me for a while if it patched up her family."

"Except it might not work that way," Larry pointed out, "and forever afterward she'd know that she could count on you to try to handle *her* business *your* way."

Vince grimaced. "I see your point, Dad, but—"

Larry lifted a hand, palm out. "No buts, son. This is where you give your own faith a real workout. God's in charge here. Let's keep it that way. I have an inkling that she'll come around when it's the right time for her to do so. If your patience gets a little test in the meanwhile, well, you must need it."

Vince's mouth crooked into a lopsided smile at the twinkle in his father's eye. "You're right. You're absolutely right. It's just that I feel so strongly that if she can't open herself up to her family again, she'll never be able to open herself completely to me."

Larry nodded sagely, saying, "Then we'll pray that way and trust God to work it out."

"And until He does, I guess I'm cooling my jets," Vince muttered with a resigned sigh.

"I don't see that you have much choice in the matter, son. She's got to resolve these issues before she can be the wife you want and need. That is what we're talking about, isn't it?"

"Yes, and I know you're right, but I'll admit that I was hoping for something else."

"I'll make a covenant with you," Larry said, placing both of his gnarled hands flat on the tabletop. "I'll pray for both of you every day until God works this thing out. In fact, let's start right now. Okay?"

Vince copied his father's posture and bowed his head. While Larry softly prayed aloud, Vince thanked God for the man sitting across from him, for the life he had led, for the wisdom to which he was privy and for not having had the sense to forward his mail.

Chapter Thirteen

Christmas rushed toward them. It spilled out of the shops and onto the sidewalks in sometimes garish displays of tattered decorations and sometimes poignant and surprising beauty. Neither moved Jolie, who had never enjoyed Christmas.

The so-called joy of the season had always eluded her. Oh, once or twice her mother had found a way to provide a modest celebration for her three children, but even the best of those memories were pretty dismal.

Jolie recalled cupcakes with sprinkles, a bitter red punch and a doll with matted hair and gaps in her eyelashes.

Once Marcus had gotten roller skates so old that the leather had been cracked, but he'd skated around their barren little apartment, careening into walls and wobbly furniture, until he'd outgrown the things. He hadn't dared skate outside for fear of the junkies and thugs who would as soon have robbed a child of his battered old skates as shoplift a candy bar.

As for Connie, she had wagged around a huge plastic piggy bank for a couple of years, and for a time they'd all scavenged coins conscientiously. Unfortunately, their cache had been raided so often that they'd never been able to fill more than the piggy's plastic feet.

Usually, their holiday gifts had been nothing more than cardboard puzzles, cheap boxes of crayons, new socks or cans of soda, if that. Sometimes the holiday had passed without anything at all to mark it. Then at the end, their mother had not even bothered to be at home.

Christmas with the various foster families had been more rewarding gift-wise, but Jolie had always felt like an outsider and a fraud at those celebrations. The gifts had never felt personal or appropriate, and she had gone out of her way to destroy more than a few of them, which she now realized had only served to make her seem ungrateful and incorrigible, as she had, in fact, been.

Since she'd reached adulthood, Marcus had routinely invited her to spend the holiday with him and his foster family, with whom he maintained a close relationship. Jolie had tagged along with him the year that she was eighteen, but not since. It hurt too much to see the easy, affectionate manner with which he and his foster family dealt with each other.

Marcus had actually found himself in a family who had truly wanted him, but they obviously hadn't wanted two mulish little girls to go along with their five boys, natural, adopted and foster. As Marcus had explained many times, she and their sister wouldn't have "fit in." She understood *now* that the house had been small, and that the boys had slept dormitory-style in one large bedroom, but she still couldn't escape the idea that Marcus's foster parents hadn't wanted her. So far as she could tell, *no one* had wanted her or Connie.

Maybe that was why Connie had latched on to Russell's low-life father, and why she, Jolie, couldn't seem to latch on to anyone at all. Until now.

She still couldn't quite fathom how it had happened, but somehow Vincent Cutler had become such a large part of her life that when Marcus called on the Tuesday following the big game to say that he and Connie and Russell would be celebrating the coming holiday at home and would like her to join them, Jolie had used Vince as an excuse.

If she hadn't been expecting Vince to call and if she hadn't had her hands full of ironing, she wouldn't even have answered the phone without checking the caller ID first. As it was, she found herself actually talking to her brother for the first time in months.

"Um, Vince probably has other plans," she said into the phone in instant reply to Marcus's rushed invitation to join him and Connie for the holiday.

It wasn't a lie; she hadn't said that Vince had plans which included *her*, but she realized now that she was hoping he did.

"Vince?" Marcus echoed. "Is that your boyfriend?"

Boyfriend. The word had a dangerous, incredulous ring to it. She took a deep breath.

"Uh, more just friend, really, and sort of my boss. Sort of. Temporarily."

Marcus seemed to brush that off. Even more surprisingly, he seemed genuinely pleased that she might have someone in her life.

"That's great, Jo! Tell me about him."

For one long, troubling moment, Jolie fought the urge to do just that, but then she reminded herself that she and Marcus weren't really on speaking terms. He had no right to know about her life.

She said flatly, "I don't think so."

"He must be good to you," Marcus surmised correctly, gently probing. "Otherwise, you wouldn't put up with him." His voice softened, lowered, then. "I've always admired that about you, Jo. You know your own worth."

"And what am I worth, Marcus?" she retorted bitterly. "Whatever it is, it doesn't make me good enough to raise a child, does it?"

"Jo, you know that's not true," he said, sounding pained. "Neither Connie or I would ever have placed Russell with you if we weren't absolutely convinced that you would be a great parent."

"Then why take him away?" she wailed.

She could feel her brother's exasperation, but his voice was mild, gentle when he said simply, "She's his mother, Jo."

"I've been more his mother than she's been!"

His voice dropped a chord, as if he didn't want to be overhead on his end.

"He's her only chance, Jo. Can't you see that?"

"He was *my* only chance!" she cried just before she hung up, but even as she said it, some part of her knew that it wasn't necessarily so. At least she was starting to believe that it might not be.

You wouldn't be coping with it alone this time.

The implications of that were breathtaking. She wanted to believe that Vince had been talking about more than friendship, but he hadn't said that. Somehow she'd gotten the feeling that his reticence had to do with her situation with her family, and that felt patently unfair to her.

Couldn't he see how she had been treated? In a very real sense, she had been used by her own brother and sister, used and then discarded.

Well, all right, not quite *discarded*, but the same as. Almost. Except she had been the one to turn her back on them, a little voice reminded her. And why shouldn't she? she countered angrily. After what they'd done, who could blame her? Why should she feel guilty about it?

She did, though. Worse, she couldn't quite deny the subtle yearning that had begun in her when she'd first heard Marcus's voice on the telephone. Yet how could she ever trust her brother and sister again? How could she bear seeing Russell and then letting him go home with them?

Suddenly she wanted two things very, very badly. She wanted to fold little Russ close, even knowing that they would take him away again afterward, and she wanted Vince to do the same with her.

When Vince showed up at the cleaners on Friday, Jolie abandoned the presser to greet him.

"Hey!" She couldn't help smiling because he was smiling, his mouth bracketed with the grooves cut by his dimples.

"Hey yourself." He leaned on the counter to talk to her. "You busy?"

She leaned backward to catch a glimpse of Mr. Geopp, who at the moment was pretending to be deaf, dumb and blind.

"I can take a minute. What's up?"

"Two things. Everybody's going bowling tonight. Want to come?"

She wondered just who "everybody" was, but the words that fell out of her mouth were, "Of course."

Dimples again.

"Excellent."

"But, um, I'm not very good," she put in quickly. "I've only tried a couple times."

"No problem."

"Oh, well, if you're sure."

He reached out and tapped the end of her nose, saying, "Absolutely positive. Now then, question number two." He briefly held up two fingers before tucking his hands into his coat pockets. "Mom wants to know if we can count on you for Christmas."

A tiny thrill mingled with relief shot through Jolie. To cover it, she glanced at the frosted window and the paper snowflakes that Mr. Geopp had taped to it.

She'd once expected to spend the holiday with Russell. Without him the whole Christmas season had seemed like a huge insult, something to be endured. She'd been dreading it more than she could even let herself admit, but since Thanksgiving she supposed that she'd been waiting for Vince to invite her to spend the holiday with him and his family.

He was like a glimmer of light at the end of what felt like a long, dark tunnel. She blinked and let her smile brighten.

"Thanks. I'm not big on Christmas really, but I'll try not to put a damper on the fun."

He chuckled. "Don't count on as much excitement as Thanksgiving. We're not expecting any new little bundles of joy. That I know of."

She laughed. "Just a humdrum Cutler holiday, hmm?"

He scratched an ear, admitting wryly, "I wouldn't count on humdrum, either."

She laughed again. "No? Really?"

He nodded in acknowledgment of the absurdity of a humdrum Cutler gathering of any type.

"The schedule usually goes something like this. Christmas eve supper around six at Mom and Dad's, followed by the reading and then the gift exchange and church at ten."

"The reading?"

"You know, the Christmas story."

"Oh, of course."

"We do it in parts so everyone gets at least one line."

"Ah."

"Anyway," he went on, "Christmas eve is the big do at our house. Mom puts on a lavish buffet for Christmas Day, and people pop in and out all day long, but Christmas eve is reserved for family. The sisters sometimes drop by on Christmas Day and sometimes don't, depending on the families of the son-in-laws. Or is it sons-in-law? I always forget."

"Sons-in-law," Jolie murmured automatically, still wondering about the reading, but it was the gift exchange thing that truly gave her pause. "Listen, Vince, I—I can't really afford…that is, there are so many of you to buy for."

He lifted a placating hand.

"Don't worry. You'd only have to buy one gift, and nobody goes overboard. We draw names because no one can buy for everybody. Mom and Dad always get together a little something for each of the grandkids, but no one else does. We do a little name-drawing ceremony that we jokingly call the family lotto. That'll be this Sunday after church. Or if you want, this year we could keep the gift thing just between the two of us."

This year. Jolie's heart kicked. This year. As if they'd be doing this again next year. As if they might actually have some sort of future together.

"I—I don't mind drawing names," she replied a little breathlessly.

"Does that mean I can count on you for church Sunday?"

She felt an unexpected spurt of eagerness. "Sure. Why not?"

He grinned. "Better and better. I'll tell Mom to expect you for dinner. We'll draw names right after."

"If you're sure it's no trouble."

"You know better than that," he told her cheerfully.

The lovely part was that she really did believe she'd be welcome.

"But, ah, there's just one thing. I-if I get you or one of the other guy's names, you'll have to give me some idea what to buy. I've never…"

"Never bought a guy gift before?"

"Only for my b-brother."

She held her breath, wondering if Vince would bring up the situation with Marcus and Connie again, but he just smiled and rocked back on his heels.

"Good. That's good."

"Is it?"

"Oh, yeah."

She couldn't account for the shyness that slipped over her then. Suddenly she couldn't quite look him in the eye any longer—not with Mr. Geopp just there on the other side of the gliding rack hung with recently cleaned garments arranged in alphabetical order according to the last name of the customer.

"Tell you what," he said, "I'll give it some thought and be prepared to dish out advice after the name-drawing. How's that?"

"That's fine." It came out almost as a croak. She cleared her throat before asking, "What time should I be ready for bowling tonight?"

"Six-thirty too early?"

She shook her head. "Gives me just enough time to get home and change."

"Then I'll pick you up at the apartment at half past six."

"Okay."

"See you then." He gave her a wave and turned to go. She wasn't really ready to let him.

"Vince?"

He swung around, as eager as a puppy.

"Yeah?"

Her heart beat so pronouncedly that it almost strangled her.

"Thank you. For Christmas, I mean."

"You bet."

"And thank your Mom for me, too."

He chuckled. "Okay. See you later."

She nodded, smiling, and he turned with a wink to pull open the door and move swiftly through it.

Jolie watched him stride down the sidewalk and out of sight, his image blurred by the frosting that had been sprayed on the window. Lifting a hand to her chest, she marveled at the way her heart had sped up at the first sight of him.

It was ridiculous, really. Just because he was handsome and kind and caring, that was no reason to over-react. Why, it was almost as if... Surely she wasn't... hadn't...

She sat down hard on the tall, three-legged stool that Mr. Geopp kept behind the counter for when his legs were aching. Her face felt flushed, and her pulse rapped a quick staccato as the truth hit her.

So this was what it felt like to fall in love.

Oh, no. This was awful!

Or so she told herself.

It didn't feel awful, actually.

It felt hopeful, so very hopeful that it was terrifying.

She closed her eyes and thought, *Dear God, oh, please don't let me be like my mother. Please don't let me be like that.*

She could almost understand now why Velma had chased after every man who had come along. She'd been chasing this feeling, this sense of hope in an otherwise hopeless life. But Vince was different from all those losers her mom had hooked up with.

Vince was good, genuinely good.

So what's he doing hanging around with you? asked that pesky little voice she'd been hearing so much from lately.

Panic swept through her. He wouldn't hang around for long. Of course he wouldn't. No one ever did, not her father, not her mother, not Russell, not one of the foster families with whom she'd lived. Why should Vince be any different? Unless...

"Oh, God," she whispered, without even knowing what she was pleading for, "Oh, God, please." And it came to her then that Vince was in her life because he wanted to be.

She hadn't pursued him, just the opposite. In fact, she'd been downright disagreeable in the beginning. Yet gradually, patiently, he'd made himself a place in her life and in so doing had worked his way into her heart.

Now she could only pray that he didn't break it.

Jolie released the ball and watched it fly down the very center of the lane, gradually straightening as it whirled nearer its target. She was a better bowler than she'd known. Then again, she hadn't had an expert like Vince to show her what she was doing wrong until now.

She backed up a step, afraid to breathe lest it affect the trajectory of the spinning ball. It plowed into the head pin, just slightly to the right of center, and sent every pin but two flying in different directions.

"You can do it," Vince called encouragingly. "It's the same spare as before. Half step to the right. You can do it."

Jolie lifted her ball from the return, scooted right and hefted the ball into place just below chest height. Taking a deep breath, she stepped off, swung her arm back, bent and released.

Once more the ball whirled straight down the alley, this time knocking out the remaining two pins. Jolie leapt straight up into the air, coming down again into Vince's arms as he had rushed forward to congratulate her. They almost toppled onto the floor, but he planted his feet and anchored them both, laughing, before releasing her.

"That's my girl!"

Jolie tried not to read too much into that while the others either applauded or groaned dramatically, depending upon which team they were on. The group consisted of Helen and John, Drew and Olivia, Donna and Martin and Vince's friend and employee Boyd and his wife, Sissy.

Neither Donna nor Helen were bowling, Donna because it was still too soon after the baby and Helen because she seemed to want to keep her sister company.

Sissy had immediately latched on to Jolie, and Jolie found that she quite liked the extremely tall, rather plain woman. Sissy was slender to the point of emaciation, though she ate like a stevedore, and had lank, dark-blond hair that hung to the bottoms of her ears on the sides and was spiked rather unflatteringly on top.

"Thyroid condition," she'd announced cheerfully as she'd consumed her second order of onion rings, having already downed a double-meat burger and a large soda.

Sissy sauntered up to bump hips and elbows with Jolie in a goofy kind of congratulatory dance, seeing as they were on the same team with Vince and Boyd. Her hip bones were like blades.

"Trust Vince to come up with the only true sportswoman in the bunch," Marty groused good-naturedly.

Sissy took issue, planting her bony hands on her bony hips. "Hey! I'll have you know that I played varsity volleyball all through high school and college."

"Now if only she could bowl," Boyd cracked with a straight-faced sigh.

"Her score's better than mine," Jolie pointed out as Sissy glowered.

Suddenly Boyd grinned and pulled his wife down onto his lap.

"I know. I just like to see her bristle."

Her long, skinny arm wound around his neck as she giggled and kicked her feet. The two were obviously mad about each other. It gave Jolie a warm, cozy feeling, especially when she felt Vince's hand slide possessively into the dip of her waist.

"Want a cola?" he asked softly.

She shook her head and leaned into him a little. Just having him close was reward enough for that spare or any other achievement she could dream up, for that matter.

He gave her a smile and asked loudly, "Whose turn is it?"

"Does it matter?" John replied drolly, getting to his feet.

"Only to the winners," Vince retorted good-naturedly.

Actually they were behind by three pins, but nobody seemed to be paying much attention to the score. It wasn't about competition. It was about fun and fellowship.

The "midnight" leagues actually started at ten o'clock, so they were out of there by nine-forty-five. Their team had lost by six pins, but the others magnanimously refrained from rubbing it in.

Marty and Donna hurried away, saying that it was time to feed the baby. Donna gave Jolie an absentminded peck on the cheek before making for the parking lot. Helen did the same, then hurried back to ask Jolie if she wanted to join the sisters for a Christmas shopping junket the next day.

"Oh, I have to work on Saturday."

"Rats," Helen said. "Well, maybe another day."

"Monday afternoons are about the only time I have," Jolie began.

"Excellent!" Helen said, "the stores won't be so crowded and we'll know whose names we've drawn by then."

"Oh, I didn't mean…that is, I'll be working at Vince's on Monday afternoon," Jolie went on apologetically. "We haven't quite finished the house."

Helen frowned. "Ah, that's okay. I just remembered that Mom can't babysit on Monday, and Donna won't leave little Tony with just anyone."

"I'll keep the baby," Vince offered.

"Really?" Helen brightened.

"But what about the house?" Jolie asked uncertainly. "We still have the library and your room to do."

"We'll do them later."

"Are you sure?"

"Absolutely. I'll even go over to Donna's place to keep the little guy there."

"It pains me to say it," Helen told him, kissing his cheek, "but you are the best big brother."

"You used to say that when I'd loan you my sweaters to wear, too," he reminded her, "then you'd return them with stains and smelling like cheap perfume."

Helen ignored that, saying to Jolie as she hurried away, "I'll talk to the others and call you."

"Does she even have my number?" Jolie wondered, waving.

"I'll give it to her," Vince said as they walked toward his truck. Obviously, he approved of her spending time with his sisters. Jolie tried not to think what that might mean. Given the gregariousness and generosity of the Cutlers, probably nothing out of the ordinary.

Olivia and Drew were the last to exit the building. They called and waved. Jolie and Vince waved back. A sleek, black, two-door coupe rumbled up beside them with Boyd hanging out the passenger-side window.

"Hey, you guys want to come over for a while? It's early still."

"Naw, us guys have to work tomorrow," Vince reminded him, "and that includes you."

"Oh, yeah, so it does," Boyd mused, playing dumb. "Oh, well, my boss is a sweetheart. He won't mind if I'm a little late."

"You just try it, mister, and I'll forget to sign your paycheck."

"In that case, I'll be there bright and early."

"Never doubted it."

Laughing, Boyd rolled up the window, his wife calling out, "See you soon, Jolie!"

"I look forward to it," she shouted at the heavily tinted window.

She and Vince stood where they were until the car pulled away.

"You wouldn't believe it to look at her, but that Sissy's an excellent cook," Vince said conversationally. "On the other hand, you might believe it looking at Boyd."

Jolie chuckled. "They're great."

"Yeah, they are. Did you know that they were high-school sweethearts?"

"So they've been together a long time then."

"Married the day after we graduated."

"But they still don't have kids?"

Vince grimaced. "It's that thyroid thing. They've always said that they would adopt when the time was right. They're looking into it now."

"I see."

"I think they'll take an older child because Boyd remembers too well what it was like to want and need a family and be passed over time and again by couples desperate for babies."

"I understand that," Jolie stated matter-of-factly, remembering all too well herself. "Marcus could have been adopted," she went on. "At least he said he could have, but it never happened."

"Wonder why?" Vince mused.

"I always figured that there was something wrong with the family he was with. They'd already adopted two other boys and had two of their own. Marcus never wanted to talk about it."

"Hmm."

They'd reached the truck, and he handed her up into it, then walked around to slide behind the wheel.

"So what are you going to shop for on Monday?" he asked, fitting the key into the ignition.

"That depends on whose name I draw and what that person wants."

He let his hand fall away from the ignition switch and half-turned to face her, one forearm draped across the top of the steering wheel. "I could tell you what I want if you're interested, but you aren't going to find it in a store."

Whatever that meant, she couldn't believe that Vincent Cutler would make an unsuitable suggestion, and she liked the idea that they might trade gifts apart from the family.

"I don't see why we couldn't exchange gifts privately," she said.

For a moment he simply stared through the windshield into the distance. Then he faced her once more.

"Jolie, I've thought about this for a long time. I've prayed about it endlessly."

"That sounds so serious," she said, trying for a light tone even though her heart had begun beating like a jackhammer.

"There's just one thing I want for Christmas," he was saying.

Could he possibly be asking for a serious relationship? she wondered wildly. Were they about to become a formal couple? Surely they were too old to go steady! But not to get engaged. The very thought left her breathless. She was ready for anything—except what he actually said.

"I want you to try to work things out with your brother and sister."

Chapter Fourteen

Jolie rocked back in her seat, feeling as if he'd sucker-punched her. *"What?"*

He repeated himself, word for word, slowly, in case she hadn't heard him the first time. "I want you to try to work things out with your brother and sister."

Anger and disappointment roared through her. How dare he? Who did he think he was to ask such a thing of her? She'd thought he cared about her!

"You don't know what you're asking!" she exclaimed.

"I know it's difficult," he said. "It may be the most difficult thing you ever do, but I believe it's so important for you that I'm willing to take this risk."

"What risk?" she snapped. "It's no risk for *you.*"

"Isn't it?" he asked softly, his smoky-blue eyes plumbing hers. Then he sighed and seemed to mentally shake himself. "You can do this, Jolie. I know you can. You're a strong, loving, intelligent woman."

She stared at him with incredulous eyes. "Why are you doing this?"

"Because I truly believe that if you don't make peace with your family, it will color the rest of your life, and I just care too much, Jolie, to let you do that to yourself. Don't you see that you have to at least try to put this pain behind you?"

She pressed her fingertips to her temples. "It seems to me that it's just adding another level of anguish to what I live with every day."

"I don't want you to live this way," he said urgently, "tied up in angry knots for the rest of your life. I certainly can't live like that."

"No one's asking you to!"

"Maybe not, but would you want it for me if it was the other way around?" he asked softly.

He knew. He knew how she felt about him! He wasn't saying it outright—obviously he didn't want to embarrass her—but he knew, And he was trying to show her that he cared for her in his own way, too, in a deeply spiritual way that he had already demonstrated over and over again. Maybe he didn't care for her the way that she wished he did, but the big, sweet lunk really did think that it would be best for her to make peace with her brother and sister.

Maybe it would. She just didn't know anymore. She closed her eyes and such a longing came over her that it was literally physical. It was a longing for the family she had lost, for the nice, normal family that she'd never quite had, and also for the family and life that only Vince himself could offer her.

"Just think about it," he urged softly. "Please, Jolie."

She *was* thinking about it; she couldn't stop thinking about it now. It was as if a hungry little something had lodged itself in the center of her chest, begging and pleading. She put a hand over her mouth. How had she gotten so needy, so weak? This was what wanting Vince in her life had done to her.

She'd been so careful not to want anyone or anything. Her whole life she'd known that to want too much was to face the bitterness of disappointment again and again, and losing Russell had just proven that. Then how could she now want Vincent Cutler? How could she not?

More importantly, what if he was right and by not doing this she would forever curtail her life in some way?

Yet, how could she work out an acceptable understanding with Marcus and Connie? There was Russell, after all. She just didn't know if she could bear to see him with anything approaching regularity and live with the knowledge that he wasn't hers, would never be hers.

Still, if trying was all that Vince asked of her, if he really thought it was best…

Doesn't it make a difference that you wouldn't be coping with it alone this time?

What if this really is best for your nephew? What if knowing his mother loves him is more important than knowing that you love him? And why shouldn't he have both?

"I'll think about it," she finally said, brushing away the tears that she only just realized were on her cheeks. "I can't promise more than that."

"I can't ask more than that," he answered, his voice thick and quivery.

She turned her face away, one hand lifting automatically to ruffle her bangs and smooth them again.

"Let's get you home," he said briskly, starting the engine. "Tomorrow's a work day."

She nodded dumbly, wondering if she was going to get much, if any, sleep that night. Dark fear and bright hope blended together within her, swirling into an ever-changing mosaic of emotions sharp enough to cut her heart to ribbons.

How ironic that in this season of peace she should feel such overwhelming inner turmoil.

Those next days were the longest of Vince's life. He couldn't sleep, couldn't concentrate.

What if he was wrong?

He didn't know Marcus or Connie Wheeler from Adam. They could be the worst sort of hateful, manipulative people. Just because Marcus was a minister didn't mean that he was trustworthy. They could break Jolie's heart all over again, just as she feared they would.

But at least she would have tried, he argued with himself. She would have done all in her power to mend the rift.

Would she, though, come out of it trusting him?

If she allowed him to push her into reconnecting with her brother and sister and then it went badly, she'd have every right to question his judgment. Worse, she might never feel for him what he felt for her.

Pushing her to make peace with her family suddenly seemed a terribly presumptuous, meddlesome, even arrogant, thing to do. He'd told himself that he was acting in her best interest, but had he acted out of selfishness instead? Oh, why hadn't he kept still and bided his time as his father had counseled him?

No longer sure of his own position, all he could do now was pray that God would guide her, give her wisdom and strength in this situation—and the ability to forgive if he was wrong about everything.

She attended church with him and his family on Sunday as planned. Afterward she joined the family for dinner. She smiled and teased and pitched in to help just like everyone else, but it all felt a little forced. She seemed brittle, shadowed, her smile honed to a fine edge. Her gaze felt guarded and diffident, as if she couldn't bear to look at anyone or anything too long, especially him.

When it came time for the family lotto, as it was jokingly called, they all gathered around the table in the kitchen.

Every year his mother baked an elaborate gingerbread display just after Thanksgiving to kick off the season, and the family had long ago incorporated the name-drawing with the gingerbread. This year as a centerpiece for the dining table, Ovida had fashioned a country church, complete with bell tower, steeple and stained-glass windows made of crushed hard candies melted into shapes and designs. For the name-drawing she had made twelve large gingerbread men and seven smaller ones, each with a name written on the back in icing that had hardened before the cookie was turned over to hide them. The children would draw for children's names from the smaller cookies, and the adults from the larger ones.

Before the actual choosing of cookies—and names—began, they all drew slips of paper with numbers printed on them to establish order. Ovida drew the number one, Vince a six, and Jolie a nine. Ovida began the game by choosing the cookie with her son-in-law John's name on it.

"Whoo-hoo! Just pack me a big box of that home-made Christmas fudge of yours," he crowed, patting his middle.

Helen goosed him playfully in the ribs. "And you told me you wanted a new nine iron."

"New iron," Ovida muttered, pretending to write that on an imaginary list. "I didn't even know you were concerned about pressing your clothes, John," she remarked innocently, knowing perfectly well that Helen had referred to a golf club and not a steam iron.

When the laughter died down, the drawing continued. Vince's turn eventually came, and he drew Sharon.

"Okay, I know just what I want," Sharon announced gleefully. She held up one hand as if admiring a ring or bracelet. "I'm thinking three karats at least."

"Three carrots," Vince drawled, borrowing his mother's joke and pretending to take notes in the air. "Would you like peas with that? Green beans maybe? A side of ham?"

"You are the ham," Sharon shot back.

More laughter followed, then Donna drew her own husband's name.

"Rats," he said good-naturedly, "and no, that's not a request, but it might as well be because I'm losing a gift in this deal."

"I'll still get you a sweetheart gift," Donna assured him, leaning into his side as she gently burped the baby on her shoulder.

Marty smiled at their child. "You already have."

"And an expensive gift it is, too," Drew quipped. "You'll be paying on it for a lifetime."

Olivia elbowed him in the ribs.

The laughter and the drawing continued.

When Jolie's turn came, she turned over a cookie bearing Vince's name.

He caught her sudden intake of breath, dimly heard the hum of speculation around them, and wondered again if he had ruined everything for them by urging her so strongly to make peace with her family. He felt the sudden need to blurt that he wanted…something, anything, a new shirt, a garden hose, a picture frame, anything at all except what he'd already said. A glance at his father had him biting back the words, but he made up his mind to take Jolie aside and tell her privately that he was wrong to stick his nose into a situation that clearly was none of his business and that she should follow her own instincts and wishes in the matter.

He never got the chance.

The right moment just never came. They were not even to have a private moment as he drove her home because as they were walking out the door, his mother asked him to drop off a casserole for an elderly friend who had difficulty cooking for herself and Olivia abruptly decided to ride along and say hello.

"You don't mind dropping me at my house after you drop off Jolie, do you, sweetie?" Olivia said, throwing on her coat.

What could he do but smile, shake his head, and tell himself that he would call Jolie later?

Later, however, she seemed to have taken the phone off the hook, because the number rang busy for over an hour before he gave up. It was getting too late to call anyway, and besides, what was the rush?

She'd be over in the morning as usual to do the laundry and work on the house before her shopping trip with his sisters. They would sit down and talk then. He would apologize for butting in, affirm her concerns and they'd be right back where they'd started.

"Oh, Father," he prayed aloud, dropping his head into his hands, "what have I done? What should I do?"

He prayed late into the night, and woke heart-heavy, no closer to certainty than before. Dragging himself out of bed and into his clothes, he went about his morning routine, making coffee and breakfast. He carried a second cup of coffee with him, sipping from it while scraping off his morning beard and combing his hair. He drained the cup before brushing his teeth, and was standing with the brush protruding from a mouth full of foam when the telephone rang.

Quickly, he rinsed and moved into the bedroom to pick up the receiver of the cordless phone beside the bed.

"Hello."

"Vince?"

He knew the instant he heard the quaver in her voice that something had happened.

"Jolie, what's wrong? You okay?"

"I—I'm not sure frankly. Can you come over?"

"Now?"

"Half an hour or so. I-it should be about that."

That didn't make a lot of sense, and when she gulped audibly, it scared the daylights out of him. He started yanking on his boots, the telephone receiver cradled between his head and shoulder.

Everything else was forgotten, especially when she added softly, "Just come over."

"I'm on my way."

He broke the connection and tossed the cordless phone onto the bed, reaching for his jacket.

All the way on the drive over, he prayed that she was all right, that he would have the wisdom and intelligence to deal with whatever had happened. He felt in his bones that it had to do with her brother and sister, and he knew that if he had caused new heartache for her they could both carry the scars of it for the rest of their lives.

Jolie opened the door and almost wilted with relief. "Thank heaven it's you."

Vince strode inside, sweeping the door closed behind him, and pulled her into his arms, holding her against his chest, her head tucked beneath his chin.

"Are you all right?"

She sighed, relishing the comfort and closeness for several seconds before gulping down the lump in her throat.

"So far. I didn't sleep much, though."

"Me, either," he rumbled. "But tell me what's happened? Why am I here?"

She took a deep breath and looked up at him.

"I spoke to my brother last night."

His reaction was not what she'd expected. Instead of breaking into a smile, Vince stepped back, his hands going to her shoulders, concern clouding his face.

"Jolie, honey, listen. I didn't mean to pressure you. It was wrong of me to meddle in something that clearly wasn't my business."

"You were just concerned for me."

"I know, but—"

Another knock at her door interrupted whatever he'd been about to say. Jolie stiffened, her heart leaping into her throat once more.

This was it then, the moment of truth. They were all about to find out just how strong and daring she was.

For Vince, she told herself, *and for Russell,* but then she was honest enough to add, *and for me.*

Drawing Vince's name had been like a message straight from heaven for her. Once she'd gotten home afterward, she'd plucked up her courage and called her brother. They'd talked for a long while, and she'd come to understand that he'd felt he'd had no choice except to do what he had—and very likely he'd been right. She couldn't blame Connie for wanting her son, and she couldn't blame Marcus for helping her gain custody of him.

In some part of her heart and mind, she'd always known that, but old emotions from the past had been reactivated by the prospect of losing physical custody of the child whom she'd come to love so much, and she'd allowed herself to lash out in pain and anger. Now with Vince on her side, she was ready to put it behind her. The only concern was Russell. She just didn't know how she would react when she saw him again.

Would the past rear its ugly head again? Or was she really ready to go forward? There was only one way to find out.

Squaring her shoulders, she put on a tremulous smile for Vince and whispered, "Merry Christmas," just before she reached for the doorknob.

He gasped and settled his hands upon her shoulders as she opened the door. The weight of them soothed and steeled her, so that she was able to greet her brother and sister with a semblance of control.

"Hello."

"Hello, Jo."

Of average height, Marcus stood just a little over three inches taller than her. He had a lean but solid look about him, and his light golden-brown hair was still damp from its morning combing. In a short while, she knew, it would begin to fall over his forehead from its straight side part as it dried. The poignant smile upon his handsome, beloved face nearly smashed her control, so she quickly glanced away.

Beside him, Connie looked pretty and petite, her golden-blond hair, now cut to chin-length, feathering softly about her face and playing up her big, muted-jade eyes. She wore a vulnerable, uncertain air, as if questioning her welcome, but it was the child in her arms who wrenched the sob up from deep inside Jolie's chest.

She clapped both hands over her mouth in an effort to prevent its escape and felt Vince squeeze her shoulders as she failed. Then Connie abruptly stepped forward and literally shoved her son into Jolie's arms.

"There's your aunt JoJo," Connie said, her voice thick with emotion. "We're so happy to see her!"

Marcus laid one hand on Connie's shoulder and reached for Jolie with the other, clasping her forearm and biting his lips as tears filled his eyes. Russell, God love him, dropped his bright red head onto Jolie's shoulder and wrapped his little arms around her. She sobbed. She couldn't help it. She was so happy to see him, to hold him!

He had grown! He felt heavier, stronger and not at all troubled by the momentous event taking place around him. Aware, yes: troubled, no.

Jolie felt an immense sense of relief. He was well, happy. Whatever they had done to one another, Russell was going to be okay because, she realized suddenly,

Russell was loved by those who should love him. What could be better for a little boy than that?

Somehow she felt...*freed* by the realization that she could truly trust this child's welfare to his mother. She hadn't expected that.

Vince lifted a hand to ruffle Russ's short, glowing, coppery locks, and Russell looked up, grinning at this friendly stranger. A watery laugh erupted from Jolie.

"Let's sit down," Vince suggested.

"Yes, let's," Connie replied brightly, blinking back tears.

Nodding, Jolie turned and led them toward the sofa with Russell in her arms.

"What a big boy you're getting to be," she murmured, surprised and delighted when he nodded his agreement. "I'm so happy to see you," she whispered.

He opened his arms wide and hugged her again.

She dropped down into one corner of the couch, Russell in her lap, as Vince introduced himself. She hadn't thought to do it herself.

"Vincent Cutler," he said simply, offering his hand to Marcus, who gave it a hearty shake.

"Jolie's mentioned you," Marcus replied. "And I'm Marcus, of course, and this is our sister Connie."

"Good to meet you," Vince said, nodding at Connie, who folded herself down onto the edge of the chair opposite the sofa.

Jolie was rubbing foreheads with Russell when Vince dropped down onto the arm of the sofa next to her.

"He looks wonderful!" she gushed to no one and everyone.

"He is wonderful," Connie said softly, "thanks to you."

Jolie swiped at her eyes, which kept leaking tears. Words just seemed to be falling out of her mouth. "I've missed him so much!"

"Oh, Jo!" Connie gasped, suddenly launching from her chair to a spot right next to Jolie. "He's missed you, too. We've all missed you. Please come back to us!"

Before Jolie could say anything to that, Connie threw her arms around her, sobbing brokenly, and then Marcus was crouching in front of them, one arm reaching out to each.

"None of us will ever be able to thank you enough for all you've done, Jo," he began, then he paused to stretch his lips tight over his teeth to control their trembling. "We never wanted to lose you, though. We just want the family back together finally. We've waited so long for that. Decades, Jo. We've waited decades to be together again. Please—" He bowed his head.

"I'm so sorry," Connie wept. "It's all my fault! If I'd been as good as you, as strong as you, none of this would have happened."

Good? Jolie thought. Strong? After wallowing in self-pity and anger all these weeks? Surely if they could overlook and forgive that, she could manage the rest. It might not be easy, but it didn't have to be as difficult as she'd been making it, either. With Russell in her lap, she gathered her brother and sister into her arms as best she could, too overcome at the moment to speak.

"JoJo," she heard Russell say, and then she felt Vince's strong, comforting hand on the crown of her head.

"Yeah, that's our JoJo," he told the boy softly, "and how blessed we all are to have her."

Jolie laughed even as she cried.

* * *

"Oh, no you don't!" Marcus exclaimed, launching off the couch to run down Russell, who'd decided that it might be fun to try to climb the curtains.

He brought the boy back dangling between his hands, which were clamped around Russell's little torso beneath his chubby arms. He plopped down on the sofa again, Russell in his lap.

"You are a little chunk."

"I can't believe how much he's grown," Jolie mused wistfully. "He was just an infant last Christmas."

"You don't even have a Christmas tree this year, Jo," Connie noted gently, folding the tissue with which she'd been dabbing her eyes.

They all seemed inclined to alternate between bouts of tears and laughter, but in Vince's estimation even the tears were happy now. *Thank You, God,* he said silently, a refrain that he had repeated over and over again as the morning had progressed.

Jolie shrugged and admitted, "I didn't see the point."

"Without Russell here," Connie surmised. "I understand."

"We had a tree last year," Jolie said quickly, and Vince realized that Connie had missed that first Christmas with her son, "but he was too little even to notice."

"He's certainly intrigued this year," Marcus said, doing his best to contain the writhing bundle of toddler energy in his lap. "We bought a four-and-a-half-footer."

"Marcus even built a nice platform for it," Connie added.

Marcus grinned wryly. "Yeah, I had this bright idea that if I made it tall enough and wide enough, he wouldn't be able to reach the tree."

"Which is true," Connie pointed out with a chuckle, "so he just climbs up onto the platform instead."

"And helps himself to the ornaments," Marcus continued.

"The whole bottom half of the tree is bare now," Connie chortled.

"And only God knows how many pine needles he's managed to swallow," Marcus confessed with a wry twist of his mouth.

"Of course, he doesn't have any understanding of Christmas yet," Connie said, mirroring Jolie's smile, "but he loves that tree."

"Tee," Russell echoed happily, kicking out with both legs in an attempt to get to the floor.

Suddenly he stopped and yawned so widely that they all laughed. With a sigh he rolled onto his side and stuck two fingers into his mouth. Connie checked her watch.

"My goodness, it's past his nap time."

Taking him from Marcus, she gathered him against her chest, rocking gently back and forth. He bucked for a few seconds, then dropped his head onto her shoulder, his sleepy eyes smiling at Jolie. Vince curled his hand around hers. It was going to be all right. Everything was going to be all right. *Thank You, God.*

"Speaking of Christmas," Marcus said, leaning forward to capture Jolie's attention. "We were hoping that this year we could all be together."

Jolie sat up a little straighter, flicking a glance sideways at Vince. "Well, I…I've already made plans."

Marcus clamped his jaw and nodded, clearly disappointed.

"That's no problem," Vince piped up, sitting forward

slightly. "The three of you will just join us at my parents' house."

Marcus and Connie traded a look. "We couldn't impose," Connie said gently.

"But you wouldn't be imposing," Vince assured her.

"That's kind of you to say," Connie told him, "but your family doesn't even know us."

"That doesn't matter," Vince said. "They'd be delighted to get to know Jolie's brother and sister."

Connie smiled, but she shook her head in refusal. Vince saw Jolie's disappointment; it was mirrored clearly in her brother's eyes.

"Marcus, won't you be spending at least part of the holiday with your foster family?" Jolie asked.

He shook his head, explaining, "Dennis has moved to Colorado with his wife and kids, and Maggie and Dad are going there this year."

"I—I thought Dennis was divorced. He's the oldest one, isn't he?"

Marcus nodded. "Yeah, they got back together. Trying to make a new start in Denver. The folks feel they really have to get behind it."

"Marcus and the other guys insisted," Connie put in.

"Well, that settles it then," Vince declared heartily, "and I won't take no for an answer. I've got to warn you, though. The place is a zoo at holiday time. You've got these two," he said to Marcus, wagging a finger between Jolie and Connie, "but I've got *four*." He held up the appropriate number of fingers in emphasis.

"*Four* sisters!" Marcus yelped.

"Hey." Connie folded her arms in mock outrage. Both men grinned.

"Two older and two younger," Vince confirmed, "which means I get it from both directions."

"Oh, they're wonderful, and you know it," Jolie scolded, slinging an elbow, which Vince easily caught. He grinned at Marcus. The two had just come to a new understanding of one another.

"Did I mention that they're all married?" Vince asked. "That's the good thing about sisters. They give you brother-in-laws."

"Brothers-in-law," Jolie and Connie both corrected.

Marcus and Vince looked at each other and burst out laughing.

"What?" Jolie asked. Connie shook her head, seeming just as mystified as Jolie. Marcus and Vince only laughed harder. "What?" Jolie demanded, finding a soft spot with her elbow this time.

Vince covered his midsection with a forearm, gasping, "It's a brother thing."

"Or rather, a sister thing," Marcus said, still grinning.

"I don't think I like that," Connie muttered, but she was grinning, too.

Marcus lifted a hand placatingly. "Now, now. What would I do without the two of you to correct my grammar?"

"And organize your life," Vince added.

"And redecorate my house," Marcus said.

"Tell me about it!" Vince hooted. "At least your sisters have good taste. Well, Jo does. I assume Connie's is similar."

"Not bad actually."

"Count yourself doubly blessed," Vince told him heartily. "My whole clan is hung up on chintz, which Jolie saved me from, by the way."

"It's not as bad as he's making it out to be," Jolie argued, seeing her brother's raised eyebrows.

"You'll see at Christmas," Vince countered, giving them a little verbal nudge. "Come on. Say you'll be there."

Marcus and Connie consulted each other with another look.

"You're sure your family won't mind?" Connie asked.

"I guarantee it," Vince stated firmly, "and if you refuse, I'll just have to have Mom and the girls badger you into it."

Marcus lifted both hands in a gesture of surrender. Jolie looked at Russell now sleeping heavily on his mother's shoulder.

"Vince has seven nieces and nephews, the youngest born on Thanksgiving Day," she told Connie. "You know Russell would love playing with all those kids."

Connie rubbed his little back. He sighed contentedly, and Connie nodded in acceptance. Vince launched into an explanation of the Cutler family's holiday schedule, and when he got to the Christmas eve church service, Marcus interrupted.

"I conduct a true midnight service, starting around eleven-thirty. Our congregation is small, but nearly everyone attends."

"Where is your church again?" Vince asked.

"Pantego."

"I don't see why we can't make both services. Ours is short. We'll go there first and join you at your church by eleven-fifteen or so."

"You could spend the night with us," Connie said eagerly to Jolie, "and be there for Russ to get his Santa gifts on Christmas morning."

"You can have my room," Marcus added encouragingly. "I'll sleep on the couch."

"Oh, no, I want her to share with me," Connie objected. She looked at Jolie again. "Remember, we always shared when we were little. I had the hardest time learning to sleep without you. It'll be like old times."

"Better," Jolie said, gripping her sister's hand. "Much better."

Vince put his head back, sighing inwardly. It wasn't the first time he'd caught himself teetering on the edge of tears that morning. Sometimes joy came with its own strings attached.

Thank You, God, he prayed again. *Thank You. Thank You.*

If he said it all day, it still wouldn't be enough.

They stood at the railing on the landing and waved one more time at Marcus, who dropped his own hand and slid behind the wheel of his small sedan, his smile still gleaming white. Jolie felt as if her heart had grown too large for her chest. If she wasn't careful she might float right up into the sky.

Pulling her cardigan tighter against the cold, Jolie turned and ambled back into the apartment. Vince followed, closing the door and propping a shoulder against it, arms loosely folded. He looked very pleased with himself. She'd allow him that.

"Thank you for inviting my family to have Christmas with yours."

"I'm looking forward to it," he said heartily.

"You're sure it'll be all right with your mom?"

"What do you think?"

She thought the Cutlers were just about the warmest, most wonderful people in the world, one in particular.

"And thank you for everything else," she said simply.

Pushing away from the wall, he walked forward and wrapped his arms around her. She laid her cheek against his chest, sighing. She'd never dreamed how lovely just being held could be.

"I am so proud of you," he said. "And you don't know how frightened I was."

"You?" She lifted her head. "Why?"

"If it hadn't worked out…" He licked his lips. "I wouldn't have blamed you for hating me."

Her jaw dropped. "Don't be silly! I could never hate you, not after everything you've done, fixing my car, working out a deal to pay for it, the maintenance agreement—"

"Which you have also paid for," he reminded her, "big-time."

She went on as if he hadn't spoken. "Thanksgiving, the game. And now this." She shook her head. "I wasn't big enough to do this without you. I'd have gone right on being mad at the world and—"

"Hush," he said. Bending his head, he gently pressed his lips to hers as if to stop the flow of her words that way.

Jolie felt her heart take flight. After a moment she drew back, studying his gaze hopefully. Dare she believe that this was more than a friendly gesture?

"Jo," he said. Cupping her face in his hands, he pressed his thumbs beneath her chin and tilted her head back. "No one's ever given me a finer Christmas present." He grinned and added, "I wonder how you'll top it next year?"

Jolie caught her breath. There it was again. *Next year.* He really must mean that they had some sort of a future together. The look in his eyes certainly seemed to say so, but how could she be sure?

"Is that a hint that I should put my thinking cap on?" she asked lightly. "Am I setting a pattern for Christmases to come here?"

He answered her with another question, his voice a deep rumble. "Is that what you want, Jolie, more Christmases to come?"

She didn't know how to answer that, wasn't even quite sure what he was asking, so she backed up a step, flapped a hand through her bangs, chuckled awkwardly. "Isn't that what everyone wants?"

"I thought you didn't particularly like Christmas."

She shrugged. "Maybe I'm learning to like it."

He laughed. "That's good to know."

She looked down. "That's not all I've learned."

"A wise person never stops learning," he told her. "Life has made you very wise, Jolie."

"I doubt it." She rolled her eyes and caught sight of the clock on the wall beside the door. "Oh, my! Your sisters are expecting to meet me at your house! We're supposed to do lunch before we hit the stores."

"Well, what are you waiting for?" he teased. "Get your coat."

She hurried to do that, thinking that the warmth she felt inside just might be all she'd ever need against a Texas December.

Chapter Fifteen

Dressed in a bright holiday sweater and a long green skirt, Ovida sported a wreath of holly in her fading red hair. She seemed as gay and giddy as the children, who were obviously on a pure sugar high, sweets grasped in their hands. Jolie felt a bit underdressed in her simple brown knit slacks, matching turtleneck and off-white cardigan, but as always Ovida immediately put her at ease, greeting her with a hug. Certainly, she welcomed Jolie and her family with all the warmth that the holiday engendered.

"Thank you so much for coming! What a pleasure to meet you. Good grief, that one could be a Cutler!" she exclaimed, rubbing a hand over Russell's bright hair. "Girls, look at this doll."

Her daughters moved forward, and Connie and Russell quickly disappeared into a gushing gaggle of Cutler sisters. Olivia broke away briefly to look over Marcus and declare him entirely too handsome for a minister.

"And single, too!" she exclaimed after a word from Connie.

That elicited a blush from Marcus and speculative remarks from the sisters. "Carolina Fowler," someone suggested suddenly.

"Or Audrey Hart."

"Wynona Phillips."

This last suggestion met a chorus of agreement.

Horrified at the obvious matchmaking, Marcus glared at Vince, who covered his laughter with a hand. Jolie shot a conspiratorial glance at Connie and found her fighting her own amusement, a rapt Russell perched upon her hip. Ovida abruptly thrust cups of hot, buttered apple cider into their hands and sent Larry after a plate of elaborately decorated sugar cookies.

This was going to be a Christmas to remember. Tomorrow would bring the delight of watching Russell's face light up when he spied his Santa toys beneath the tree in Marcus's living room, but tonight belonged to the Cutlers.

As usual, it was chaos, exuberant, delightful chaos, and Jolie loved it. She loved everything at the moment. In fact, she'd never been happier.

The last eleven days had been among the brightest and busiest of her life. Between work, finishing Vince's house—she'd wanted it done in time to decorate for the holiday since it was his first in his new home—and getting reacquainted with her family, the days had flown by in a happy blur, much like the children who ran through the room to the flash of John's camera as he wandered around, capturing the celebration on film.

He snapped Larry shaking hands with Marcus, then paused long enough to copy the greeting, while the other brothers-in-law lined up to follow suite.

Smiling, Jolie looked around her.

The Christmas tree, which had gone up in the living room on the day after Thanksgiving, was surrounded by a miniature mountain range of colorfully wrapped gifts. A cheery blaze flickered in the brick fireplace, and carols wafted softly from speakers placed around the lavishly decorated house. Stuffed angels, handsewn of patterned chintz (of course) and decorated with wisps of organza, velvet, lace and sequins, with yarn for hair, were tucked into every available corner and niche. Vince and Marcus had traded rueful glances over that small fact.

Within minutes of their arrival, the newcomers were all laughing and talking with clusters of the Cutler family as if they'd known one another for ages. Eventually, Bets took center stage, clapping her hands and stomping her feet until she got everyone's attention.

"It's time. It's time," she announced, sounding very adult. "And I want to be Mary!"

"I get to be Elizabeth!" her cousin Brenda announced.

"Tony's Baby Jesus!" one of the boys shouted.

"An honorary role only," his father admonished the infant teasingly.

"Time to read the Christmas story," Vince explained as he escorted Jolie to the hearth, where they perched side by side on plump chintz (what else?) pillows.

The other adults began sorting themselves into seats, couple by couple, more than half on the floor, as Ovida passed out folios bound in red and green construction paper and decorated with bits of rick rack and ribbon. She handed one to Marcus, who took up a spot on the floor next to Jolie, his back to the long, brick hearth.

"You'll read Zacharias for us, won't you, Pastor Wheeler?"

"My pleasure," Marcus said, "but please use my given name."

"Marcus, then." She smiled before turning to her husband. "Daddy, you'll be the narrator. Mark, you're Herod. Matthew, Michael, shepherds."

Connie wound up on a chair next to Donna and Marty, who held baby Tony against his shoulder. Ovida must have handed out a dozen of the bound scripts before passing around simple stapled copies to the others. Jolie and Vince got one to share. Jolie saw immediately that the story was taken from several books of the Bible since the passages were denoted in the margins.

When everyone had settled down, Larry cleared his throat, opened his copy and began to read what was obviously a familiar and beloved story. It began with an encounter between Zacharias and an angel who announced the coming birth of a son for the elderly priest and his previously barren wife, Elizabeth. That child would turn out to be John the Baptist, cousin and forerunner of Christ. Jolie listened and followed along, fascinated. Everyone, she mused, knew the story of the Baby Jesus, but she'd never before heard this part.

The reading, some of which was very dramatic and moving, took all of forty minutes, and when it was done, Jolie marveled at the extent of what she had not known, the fulfillment of prophecy, including the flight into Egypt and Herod's murder of the male children in an attempt to remove any king of the Jews who might one day challenge him for power. No one had ever mentioned to her, for instance, the encounters of Simon and the prophetess Anna with the Holy Infant in the temple.

There was so much more to the story than she had

realized! She determined to give the Biblical accounts a careful reading at the first opportunity, including the Old Testament prophecies. It was one of these with which the reading ended, a quotation from the ninth chapter of Isaiah, verse six.

"And His name will be called Wonderful Counselor, Mighty God, Eternal Father, Prince of Peace."

With those final words, a moment of reflective silence descended. Marcus closed his script reverently.

"This is really marvelous," he said. "It's straight from Scripture, but I don't think I've ever seen it arranged so clearly. Could I possibly have a copy to share with my congregation?"

"Take mine," Vince said, handing over his white paper copy.

Bets leaned forward with a mischievous gleam in her eye. "Since we're giving away stuff, can *I* have my presents now?" she asked witheringly.

Laughter and a mild scolding followed, but Larry ultimately made the decision. "Everyone can have their gifts *after* we pray." The whole group quieted, and Larry looked to Marcus. "Would you like to lead us?"

"Oh, no," Marcus answered immediately. "Surely that honor must fall to you."

Larry didn't protest, merely bowed his head and began to speak. He finished by saying, "Most of all, I thank You, Father, for the special ways You've moved in the lives of our family this holiday season. You've always blessed us with amazing and undeserved generosity. You cleanse our souls and mend our hearts, and for that most of all we praise You. Now make us agents of Your love in this season of love and always. These things we pray in the holy name of Your Son. Amen."

"Amen," Jolie whispered, turning her gaze on Vince. He smiled benignly and squeezed her hand before popping up to help the children distribute the gifts.

All of the adults had at least a single gift to open. Due to the so-called "sweetheart" gifts, most had two, as did each of the children, one as a result of the "family lotto" and the other from their grandparents. Ovida and Larry had been good enough even to provide a gift for Russell, as had Jolie. She'd wanted Vince to have something under the tree, too, so she'd bought him a hand-tooled leather cover for his Bible and sent it along with his sisters after their shopping trip. Jolie herself had several gifts waiting for her, one from Sharon, who had drawn her name, and one each from her brother, sister and nephew.

In addition to this bounty, the grown Cutler children had joined together to buy a gift for their parents. This seemed to be a yearly event, and this Christmas the gift was a large-screen television that the sons-in-law carried in from the garage where they'd hidden it earlier. Clearly, Larry was delighted.

"The Super Bowl Party is here this year!" Drew announced, but Vince immediately objected.

"No way. I got my big screen last week, so I've got first dibs. It's already agreed."

"You've agreed," Donna pointed out. "Jolie hasn't."

Jolie glanced around in surprise. "It's not up to *me*."

Obviously that was so, because the matter died instantly. Donna wasn't even looking at Jolie anymore. Instead, she was taking Tony from her husband, and saying something to Connie. Vince had gone back to directing the opening of the gifts.

All the gifts had two tags attached to them, one of

which had been removed and deposited into a large glass bowl as the packages were passed out. It was Vince's job to draw the tags, one by one, and announce the name to the assembly. That person could then open the gift of his or her choice, saving the other for next draw. The fun part was the anticipation of hearing one's own name and the absolute delight that everyone seemed to take in watching one another open gifts.

Jolie's name was called early on, and she first chose a package from Marcus. It was a new Bible bound in supple tan leather with pages edged in gold. Inside, he had written an inscription. "To Jolie, one of the two dearest sisters in the world. May God bless you with every good thing, shelter you from harm and fill your life with love. Marcus."

She hugged him and treasured his whispered, "I love you, sis."

"I love you, too."

Next time around, she opened Connie's gift, a touching photo album filled with old pictures of them as children and recent ones of Russell, Connie and Marcus. They spent several minutes with their heads together, looking through the pages, remembering and laughing as they'd done as children.

"I can't believe you managed to save these," Jolie said, brushing her fingertips across a sheet of old photos.

"I can't believe I have my sister back," Connie said softly, blinking away tears.

Jolie trumped her handily. "I have my sister, my brother and my nephew."

"Wanna trade?" Olivia cracked, lightening the mood and making everyone laugh.

"No, thank you," Jolie replied smoothly, widening her eyes as if in horror.

Everyone laughed again. Vince put a stop to it by plunging his hand back into the bowl. Some time later he finally drew his own name.

Even though he'd said he only wanted to see her reunited with her family, Jolie hoped he'd like her other gift. He broke the ribbon, ripped away the wrapping paper and lifted off the top of the box, batting back the tissue inside. For a moment he simply stared at the leather Bible cover handstitched and dyed with a Western motif and embossed with his name. Then he smiled, reached out for her and, to her mingled embarrassment and delight, kissed her soundly on the mouth before showing off his gift to the company at large. Larry especially seemed to like it. He examined the cover in detail, murmuring that it was "Neat."

"Thanks, babe," Vince said. "I wasn't expecting that." He slid her an apologetic look and added, "Guess I should've put something under the tree for you, too."

"Oh, that's all right," she said.

She hadn't expected anything from him, certainly not a "sweetheart" gift as it was termed. It would have been nice, true, but she looked at Russell, saw how engrossed he was with the stacking blocks she'd given him and recognized the understanding smiles on the faces of her brother and sister. It was enough. How could she ask for more?

With his free hand, Vince drew another name and another and another. Eventually Jolie opened her gift from Russell. It was a framed photo of him. He'd been allowed to scribble on the mat with a crayon, which set off the photo charmingly. And finally she unveiled the beautiful silk-blend sweater from Sharon.

"This is beautiful!"

"It's the very color of your eyes," Sharon told her proudly.

Jolie looked at the lovely green sweater and beamed.

When the last gift had been opened, pronounced delightful and appropriately envied, Vince turned over the bowl as a demonstration of its emptiness and placed it on the floor.

"Guess that's it, folks. Pretty good haul, eh?"

General statements of agreement followed. Bets noted that the children still had Santa gifts to look forward to, and her parents teased her about the possibility of her only receiving coal and switches. She didn't seem very worried.

Jolie rose to help Sharon begin gathering up the trash, but Vince stopped her with a hand on her wrist.

"Wait a minute," he said rather loudly, drawing a small gold-foil bag from his jacket pocket. "Looks like we have one more gift, after all."

Jolie laughed, sure that the pretty gold-foil bag was for her, and sank back down onto the hearth next to Connie, who had squeezed in earlier while looking at the photo album. She couldn't help feeling a little thrill because Vince had bought something for her, after all, not a *sweetheart* gift, of course, but it was enough that it was personal.

Marcus left Russell playing happily on the floor and eased up onto the corner of the hearth next to Connie.

Vince placed the small bag in Jolie's hand, and she felt something hard and cubic inside. Pulling the bow from the fringed draw string, she emptied the sack of its contents. A small, white velvet box tumbled onto her lap, just the right size for a ring.

Jolie immediately dismissed the crazy possibility that popped into her mind. It couldn't be. She'd let her own wishful thinking completely run away with her. And yet… Her heart was beating pronouncedly as she looked to Vince for some clue as to what she would really find inside that tiny box. The glow in his eyes literally took her breath away.

"Oh, no!" she gasped.

Chapter Sixteen

Vince felt his heart plummet to the pit of his stomach. He'd been so sure. Christmas eve, surrounded by her family and his, had seemed the perfect moment. But now…well, there was no backing out now. His whole family knew what he was planning.

He blew out a deep breath, slipped off the hearth, crouching before her, and reached for the jeweler's box in her lap. She hadn't yet touched it. Her hands hovered about her shoulders, as if she feared the thing would bite her.

More likely it would bite him.

Mentally whispering a quick prayer, he closed his hand around it, dropped that hand to his side and murmured softly, "Am I refused before I've even asked, then?"

What was he going to say to his family? They all expected a happy announcement. Jolie clapped both hands over her mouth as if to say that wasn't going to happen.

"Guess I'm not as clever as I thought I was," Vince said with a self-deprecating grimace. He tried for a smile and failed miserably. "That's what I get, going for the grand romantic gesture."

He cleared his throat and would have risen if she hadn't reached out to capture his face in both her hands, forcing his gaze to hers. Tears shimmered in her eyes, eyes that brimmed to overflowing. With love.

And disbelief.

"This can't be happening," she said in a tiny, shaky voice. "Not to *me*."

Vince tilted his head and felt the tremble of her fingers against his skin. Hope blossomed, the hope that he had misunderstood her initial reaction.

"Why not to you?" he asked patiently, aware that everyone else in the room seemed to be holding their collective breath.

Jolie gave her head a truncated shake. "I'm not the sort of person who...we're not like you." She waved a hand broadly, looking up at the arrested assembly. "Cutlers are...you're *normal*."

Relief washed through Vince, relief mingled with a shade of irritation.

"Whatever that is," he snapped. Then he reached for his patience. "Normal is one of those things that can't be easily defined, but all right, so you're not like us. So what? I wouldn't want you if you were."

Only the instant the words left his mouth did he realize how true they were.

Okay, she'd had issues that had needed settling, relationships that had needed mending, but that didn't mean that he wanted her to change who she was. He loved her as she was. She was perfect for him as she was. Why hadn't he told her that earlier?

He sighed, realizing that he'd handled this whole

thing badly. Bowing his head, he quickly prayed for God to give him the right words.

"We're blessed, we Cutlers," he began, trusting God to put the words into his mouth. "We've had nice *normal* lives, wise, caring parents. God must have known that we couldn't handle anything else. Or maybe He was just preparing me for you, the way He was preparing you for me." He fitted his hand around the gentle curve of her jaw, feeling a certain peace, a rightness settle over him. "He gave you a special kind of strength, Jo. You've never had a stable home life, parents who protected and guided you, and yet you're one of the best people I know."

"I'm *not*," she insisted tearfully. "I've been so selfish, so angry."

"So human," he amended. "Honey, the shocker is not that you've had negative emotions as a result of negative experiences, it's that you continue to be so caring, so honorable, so forgiving, so solidly, stubbornly *you*."

"That sounds like the sort of man *you* are," she told him wonderingly, "not the sort of woman *I* am."

"Do you know what sort of woman *you* are, Jolie?" he asked, and then he answered his own question. "You are exactly the sort of woman I need, exactly the sort I could love for the rest of my life if you'll just— Whoa!"

She nearly bowled him over, flying off the hearth and throwing her arms around his neck.

He dropped the box to the floor and caught himself with one hand. Laughter rushed up out of his throat as he steadied them both. He heard gasping and sniffles in the background and the sweetest squeaking in his ear.

"I love you so much!"

Now they were getting somewhere. He hugged her tightly for a moment, torn between elation and relief.

"Let's try this again. Okay?"

"O-o-kay," she managed.

Easing her back onto the hearth, he groped for the box with one hand. At the same time, he was having some trouble getting her to let go of him, but he managed it with little squeezes and pats and tugs. She quaked all over, like the first leaf of spring meeting the last icy blast of winter. He felt a sharp tap on his shoulder. Looking up, he found his precocious niece at his side.

Bets grinned down at him and shoved her hand at his face. On her palm, just beneath his nose, rested the white velvet box that had started all of this. Trust Bets to get herself into the spotlight.

He picked up the tiny box between his thumb and forefinger, saying wryly, "Thanks."

She inclined her head, grinning, spun on her tiptoes and paraded back to her seat, her hands clasped behind her.

"I would make a very good flower girl, by the way," she announced cheekily.

Laughter sputtered, eddied, faded while Vince hung his head in mock chagrin.

Bets had temporarily upstaged him, but he knew who held the major roles. Now it was time for this little drama to reach its climax.

Taking a deep breath, he rocked forward onto one knee, reached out and clapped a hand around the nape of Jolie's neck, steadying both of them and feeling her lovely hair slide beneath his fingers. She had worn it down, a simple rhinestone clip at one temple.

Plain and simple, that was Jolie.

No, not plain.

She had to be one of the most beautiful women in the world, and—incredibly—she was meant for him. He knew it at the very core of his being, and that certainty gave him strength, peace, joy.

"Jolie Kay Wheeler," he said in a firm, even voice, "will you marry me?"

She made a strangled noise and burst into tears. His heart stopped again, then Marcus grabbed his hand and began pumping it while Connie hugged her sister comfortingly.

"Hang on. Hang on," Vince instructed, wanting this thing settled in no uncertain terms. She hadn't actually said yes yet.

He dropped the box into Jolie's hands. She stared at it for a moment and then began wrenching at it, sobbing or laughing, he couldn't tell which. Impatiently, he snatched the box back, snapped it open and plucked out the ring, holding it up so that the two narrow, red satin ribbons that he'd attached to the band hung down in front of her.

This time, he was sure that it was laughter which shook her. Smiling, he explained himself.

"It comes with strings attached."

"Yes," she said, scrubbing at the tears on her face.

Since he wasn't exactly sure what that meant, he proceeded, lifting one thin ribbon with an index finger.

"This one is love."

She giggled. Jolie, his Jolie, actually *giggled*.

"You have to say it so everyone else can hear it," he instructed around a smile.

"Yeah, otherwise nobody'll believe it," Marty cracked.

Everyone laughed, the sound rich and ebullient.

"I love you!" Jolie declared to mild applause.

Vince was having a really good time now. He hadn't done so badly, after all. He lifted the second ribbon.

"This one is marriage."

Another wave of applause washed through the room as Jolie reached for the ring, but Vince was determined to hear it plainly said, so he jerked the ring back. She caught the tail end of the ribbon, and for a moment they performed a little tug of war. Something told him that it wouldn't be the last.

He couldn't have been happier. God knew he'd be bored inside of a week with a meek, compliant little mouse of a woman. Besides which, the other Cutler women would eat her alive! A prickly, sassy, strong-willed but good-hearted female was exactly what he needed, and even she seemed finally to know it.

"You knucklehead," she said, sniffing, "of course I'll marry you."

The room erupted, as did Vincent's heart. Jolie yanked the ring out of his grasp and threw her arms around him again. He caught her against him, rocking her wildly as blows of congratulations rained down on his shoulders.

Connie sat on the hearth, openly weeping and laughing, her son standing at her knees, while Marcus was on his feet, shaking hands and accepting congratulations as if he was the bridegroom.

Suddenly Vince felt himself close to tears. Jolie seemed to know it instantly.

She pulled back far enough to place her forehead against his and whisper, "I do love you, Vince, with all my heart."

"I know that," he said, hugging her tight once more,

"but it's no more than I love you. We're going to be so happy, Jo."

After a moment, they both sank back onto their heels. Vince took the ring, admiring the single, brilliant-cut diamond—not *too* large because Jolie wouldn't like anything ostentatious—and slipped it onto her finger, ribbons and all.

It was a tight fit with the ribbons still attached, but he wasn't ready to remove them just yet. He'd tie them around her wrist if he could. Or his own. He settled for cupping her face in his hands and kissing her firmly.

His sisters were planning the wedding aloud in the background.

"Valentine's Day," he heard Olivia say.

"It's perfect," Donna declared.

Vince climbed to his feet, taking Jolie with him, his anxious gaze on her face, but she put her head back and laughed, saying, "Don't look at me. I'm not about to get in the way of that."

Vince relaxed, Jolie's hand clutched tightly in his, and half teased, "I'm counting on you to keep them from decking me out in ruffles and a red tuxedo."

"On the budget you've given us?" Sharon scoffed. "We'll be lucky if we can get *her* properly outfitted."

"Oh, wait!" Helen exclaimed, rushing over to spin Jolie around and take her measure with a critical eye. Abruptly she nodded. "Mother," she announced, "Jolie can wear your dress."

"That old thing?" Ovida gasped, but even Vince could hear the delight in her voice. "It's from the sixties, Empire waistline, little wedding ring collar, straight skirt."

"And sleeveless," Sharon pointed out. "In February."

"We'll get a little lace jacket," Donna suggested eagerly. "No, velvet, white velvet. Simple, sleek, elegant."

Jolie literally clapped her hands, eyes bright, the lines of her face softened with happiness and laughter.

Suddenly, Vince couldn't contain his joy a moment longer. He wrapped his hands around her waist, lifted her and literally spun her in a circle.

The Cutlers were big on celebration, big on family, big on faith and big on love. Their collective past was glorious with holiday memories and shared joys, but this was surely a year that would stand out among all the rest. A Thanksgiving baby, a Christmas engagement, hopes and dreams fulfilled. A perfect, God-given love.

Dear Reader,

Have you ever forgotten to have your mail forwarded or change an address? I certainly have, and the experience impressed upon me the knowledge that God does indeed move in mysterious ways. I'm always amazed at the many, many ways He uses to touch us. He can and does employ unusual and profound circumstances to work in our lives, but He also uses the small, mundane, often irritating, everyday matters, too.

It's not just a matter of circumstance, though. God uses people, thankfully. I earnestly hope, in some small way, to be one of them. And I want each of my readers to know that by the simple act of picking up one of my books and spending time with it, you have made yourself a blessing to me.

So seldom do we actually deserve the rewards and blessings that God heaps upon us that we too often turn a blind eye to them, certain that such largesse is not meant for us and unwilling to be disappointed by expecting too much. Yet, when we first seek to learn the ways of God, we begin to become acquainted with His boundless love. Only by learning that happy lesson are we able to truly receive all that He has in store for us.

So, once more, here's to love.

God bless,

Arlene James

Take 2 inspirational love stories FREE!

PLUS get a FREE surprise gift!

Mail to Steeple Hill Reader Service™

In U.S.
3010 Walden Ave.
P.O. Box 1867
Buffalo, NY 14240-1867

In Canada
P.O. Box 609
Fort Erie, Ontario
L2A 5X3

YES! Please send me 2 free Love Inspired® novels and my free surprise gift. After receiving them, if I don't wish to receive anymore, I can return the shipping statement marked cancel. If I don't cancel, I will receive 4 brand-new novels every month, before they're available in stores! Bill me at the low price of $4.24 each in the U.S. and $4.74 each in Canada, plus 25¢ shipping and handling and applicable sales tax, if any*. That's the complete price and a savings of over 10% off the cover prices—quite a bargain! I understand that accepting the books and gift places me under no obligation ever to buy any books. I can always return a shipment and cancel at any time. Even if I never buy another book from Steeple Hill, the 2 free books and the surprise gift are mine to keep forever.

113 IDN DZ9M
313 IDN DZ9N

Name	(PLEASE PRINT)	
Address	Apt. No.	
City	State/Prov.	Zip/Postal Code

Not valid to current Love Inspired® subscribers.

Want to try two free books from another series?
Call 1-800-873-8635 or visit www.morefreebooks.com.

Love Inspired

TITLES AVAILABLE NEXT MONTH

Don't miss these four stories in November

LOVING TENDERNESS by Gail Gaymer Martin
Part of the LOVING miniseries

After her car broke down, Hannah Currey was relieved when caring stranger Andrew Somerville helped her find refuge. His gentle attention helped her believe in love again. But with a painful secret haunting her, would Hannah be able to return the love this one-in-a-million man so deserved?

HER CHRISTMAS WISH by Kathryn Springer
Tiny Blessings

Little Olivia wants a new mommy for Christmas, and she's got just the person picked out. Who could be more perfect than her new nanny, Leah? After all, her widowed father's been smiling more since Leah started. Will Olivia get her Christmas wish?

JOY IN HIS HEART by Kate Welsh

Joy Fuller knew she couldn't marry Brian Peterson. He wanted a society wife, not a tomboyish pilot. That's what Joy told herself when they broke up. Now, twelve years later, they're thrown together on a rescue mission. And if they can stop quarreling, they might realize they're still hopelessly in love.

IN THE SPIRIT OF...CHRISTMAS by Linda Goodnight

As December approached, Christmas tree farm owner Lindsey Mitchell desperately needed assistance. She hired widower Jesse Slater, who fit right in...except when it came to holiday spirit. Can Lindsey teach him and his adorable daughter the true meaning of Christmas?

LICNM1005